NEIGHBOU

CLAUDE HOUGHTON OLDFIELD was born in 1889 in Sevenoaks, Kent and was educated at Dulwich College. He trained as an accountant and worked in the Admiralty in the First World War, rejected for active service because of poor eyesight. In 1920 he married a West End actress, Dulcie Benson, and they lived in a cottage in the Chiltern Hills. To a writers' directory, Houghton gave his hobbies as reading in bed, riding, visiting Devon and abroad, and talking to people different from himself. He added: "I like dawn, and the dead of night, in great cities." He disliked fuss, noise, crowds, rows, and being misquoted, or being told how much he owed "to some writer I've never read."

Houghton's earliest writing was poetry and drama before turning to prose fiction with his first novel, *Neighbours*, in 1926. In the 1930s, Houghton published several well-received novels that met with solid sales and respectable reviews, including *I Am Jonathan Scrivener* (1930), easily his most popular and best-known work, *Chaos Is Come Again* (1932), *Julian Grant Loses His Way* (1933), *This Was Ivor Trent* (1935), *Strangers* (1938), and *Hudson Rejoins the Herd* (1939). Although he published nearly a dozen more novels throughout the 1940s and 1950s, most critics feel his later works are less significant than his novels of the 1930s.

Houghton was a prolific correspondent, generous in devoting his time to answering letters and signing copies for readers who enjoyed his books. One of these was novelist Henry Miller, who never met Houghton but began an impassioned epistolary exchange with him after being profoundly moved by his works. Houghton's other admirers included his contemporaries P. G. Wodehouse, Clemence Dane, and Hugh Walpole. Houghton died in 1961.

MARK VALENTINE is the author of several collections of short fiction and has published biographies of Arthur Machen and Sarban. He is the editor of *Wormwood*, a journal of the literature of the fantastic, supernatural, and decadent, and has previously written the introductions to editions of Walter de la Mare, Robert Louis Stevenson, L. P. Hartley, and others, and has introduced John Davidson's novel *Earl Lavender* (1895), Claude Houghton's *This Was Ivor Trent* (1935), Oliver Onions's *The Hand of Kornelius Voyt* (1939), and other novels, for Valancourt Books.

NEIGHBOURS

CLAUDE HOUGHTON

With a new introduction by
MARK VALENTINE

VALANCOURT BOOKS

Neighbours by Claude Houghton
First published London: Robert Holden, 1926
First Valancourt Books edition 2014

Copyright © 1926 by Claude Houghton Oldfield
Introduction © 2014 by Mark Valentine

Published by Valancourt Books, Richmond, Virginia
Publisher & Editor: James D. Jenkins
20th Century Series Editor: Simon Stern, University of Toronto
http://www.valancourtbooks.com

isbn 978-1-941147-08-5 (trade paperback)

Set in Dante MT 11/13.2
Cover by M. S. Corley

INTRODUCTION

Claude Houghton was thirty-seven years old when his first novel, *Neighbours*, was published in 1926. His full name was Claude Houghton Oldfield and he was born in Sevenoaks, Kent, in 1889, and educated at Dulwich College (Raymond Chandler was a contemporary there, and its other scholars included P. G. Wodehouse, A. E. W. Mason and Dennis Wheatley). He trained as an accountant, and worked in the Admiralty in the First World War, rejected for active service by poor eyesight. In 1920 he married a West End actress, Dulcie Benson, and they lived in a cottage in the Chiltern Hills.

To a writers' directory, Houghton gave his hobbies as reading in bed, riding, visiting Devon and abroad, and talking to people different to himself. He added: "I like dawn, and the dead of night, in great cities." He disliked fuss, noise, crowds, rows, and being misquoted, or being told how much he owed "to some writer I've never read". Those whose influence he did acknowledge included Swedenborg, Balzac, Flaubert and "the great Russian novelists": ambitious models which reveal the seriousness with which Houghton took his writing.

Though it was his first published novel, *Neighbours* was not his first literary work. He had issued, sometimes at his own expense, three volumes of verse and two verse plays, and a book of essays on spiritual themes, *The Kingdoms of the Spirit* (1924). He was also a contributor to theosophical and occult journals. It would be fair to say that, until his later acclaim as a novelist, these early books went largely unregarded. They were earnest, soulful, but their form, elevated and orotund, was already out of date. Nothing in them, apart perhaps from a certain intensity and a deep conviction concerning the meshing of the cosmic and the material worlds, offered any suggestion that here was a writer who would soon move minds and startle imaginations.

Houghton had some trouble getting his novel published. Given its themes, which have strong erotic, psychological and metaphysical aspects, it would take a bold publisher to accept it. Grant Richards, veteran of the fin de siècle, publisher of Arthur Machen, Ronald Firbank, M. P. Shiel and others at the outré edges of literature, would have liked to take it, and had indeed issued Houghton's *The Tavern of Dreams, A Volume of Verse* in 1919, probably the best of his work from this pre-novel period in Houghton's career. But Richards was in one of his periodic publishing crises. Nevertheless, he gave Houghton every encouragement, and may have acted as a sort of agent for the book: the author later told him "you did so much for the book". In the event, it was a young and energetic imprint, Robert Holden, who gave Houghton his chance.

This publisher had already scored successes with Russell Thorndike's swashbuckling tale of smuggling in Kent, *Dr Syn*, and several of the rather racy occult romances of Charlotte Mansfield, such as *The Green Ghost* (1922). In the same year as *Neighbours* the firm also published a book of fantasies by the young Melbourne (Australia) fantasist Vernon Knowles (*Here and Otherwhere*, 1926) and the Irish bohemian Brigit Patmore's *This Impassioned Spectator*, a book of three stories about the "funny and damned" love between Bright Young Things, unusually condemned by a critic for "too much fine writing". The title and theme might almost have applied to Houghton's novel.

But in its form, an intensely written journal of emotions and convictions, and its sustained, morbid power, *Neighbours* was certainly quite unlike any other novel of the time. It is an erotically-charged study of a dual personality, a sort of psychological doppelgänger story. The protagonist, taking an attic room high above London, records in minute detail the artistic and sexual affairs of another lodger, in rooms opposite. This character, a fevered and fervent would-be author, is passionately evoked, suggesting he is partly autobiographical.

As the book unfolds, the reader feels uneasy about the obsessive voyeurism of the narrator. But then the realisation grows that we are really witnessing something else, and we begin to wonder about the exact relationship between the staid, dulled observer who is our narrator, trapped in the world of appearances, and his neighbour, the fervent, flaming visionary soaring too high towards the sun. The denouement is not entirely unforeseen but is still a masterly stroke of ambiguity, strongly conveyed and thought-provoking. It provides the pattern for many of Houghton's subsequent books, in which we only see the central character through the eyes of others, and we are left at the end with an enigma and yet a conviction of a profound allegory in play.

The book was noticed, but there is a sense that critics hurried by it a little, as too strong to be sure about: was it a work of a genius, still somewhat crude in his effects, or was it an odd, interesting failure by a literary eccentric? A provincial review noted that the book was one of those that compel interest "almost against the reader's will" and that it was "a weird story" about "a literary recluse in the attic": true up to a point, but possibly missing the book's deeper intent. The *Spectator* reviewer (18 December 1926) was one of those who supposed, not unnaturally, that the author was young, and observed that his book was: "three-quarters talk—talk about Time and Space and Eternity, the meaning or meaningless-ness of life, the wickedness of convention, the relative places of man and woman. It is very shocking. It is hopelessly unreal. The characters all speak as though they were intoxicated, and the book shows a youthful preoccupation with the subject of madness. Mr. Houghton has blown off a great blast of steam: and has proved himself to possess considerable talent."

The notice went on to hope that Houghton would write another book "more true to life". The critic cannot perhaps be blamed for failing to see the balance Houghton was trying to achieve between lives in all their desperate actuality and the unseen forces and ema-nations working through them. "In all things there is mystery," Houghton had written in *The Kingdoms of the Spirit*, "and the great-est mystery we can approach is the soul of man". In his first novel he was trying by allegory to depict the complexities and passions of the soul of an artist and visionary. It was a bold, ardent and vigorous attempt, and Houghton was later to admit that it was not quite a novel—his second, *The Riddle of Helena* (1927) was, he told Richards, "in one sense, my first", meaning, I think, that *Neighbours* was really in a different form, a sort of odyssey of the soul.

Houghton himself noted, in the same letter to Grant Richards, that *Neighbours* "may have suffered at birth from the success of

Dusty Answer". This first novel by Rosamund Lehmann also had strong (for the time) bohemian, artistic and erotic content, and had become something of a scandal, and a touchstone for the Twenties "lost generation". Houghton noted that it had been made Book of the Month and hastened to add that it was "[a] success richly deserved in my judgement". But he evidently thought that it had left little room for his own book to make an impact, and also that the success of Lehmann's book had taken all the attention of his own American publisher, Elliot Holt.

It took four more years before acclaim came for Houghton's fiction, with the great success of his *I Am Jonathan Scrivener* (1930, also available from Valancourt), a work, like *Neighbours*, with a labyrinthine mystery at its heart and a great question-mark over its ending, which either strikes readers as the only apposite climax, or infuriates them so much, that in the words of one, they simply want to throw the book across the room. Before this vogue success, Houghton had been so hard up in trying to make a living as a writer, that he resorted to doing hackwork "books of the film" for the Readers Library, starting with *The Last Command* in 1929.

But after *I Am Jonathan Scrivener*, Houghton enjoyed a period of about ten years when his books were in demand, his themes were taken seriously, and he was reviewed with wary respect. He was still an odd man out in English literature: his novels were an uneasy mixture of thriller and mystery themes—murder, suicide, disappearance, betrayal—with contemporary preoccupations—all the turmoil of the interwar years—all presented as great metaphysical dramas, with characters that, if not exactly gods, were certainly strange angels or masked archons. It was a very heady mix: possibly the only remote comparison would be with Wyndham Lewis's satires and afterlife fantasies, beginning with *The Childermass* (1928).

The critic Geoffrey West in *The Bookman* for November, 1932 noted that Houghton had still not had all the attention he deserved, "as one of the two or three most profoundly imaginative writers of his generation". He first enumerated his weaknesses: "He can be gaudy in description, at times merely clever in dialogue" and is sometimes over-ambitious, his effects daring long-shots that only just about succeed. But all his work, West says, is written from

a "spiritual—though never doctrinal—conviction". His characters
are on "an inward Odyssey" towards a revelation of the true nature
of the world. The turmoil of the time he was writing, the Thirties,
with its mass unemployment, depression, political extremism, the
rattling of the chains of the dogs of war, Houghton attributes
in part to the lack of spiritual maturity. West quotes a "gnomic
phrase" used by Houghton that he says is a keynote of all his books:
the maxim of Novalis that "Where no gods are, spectres rule". To
understand it fully, says the critic, one must read the books.

Amongst his most successful novels in this period were *Julian
Grant Loses His Way* (1933) and *This Was Ivor Trent* (1935, also
available from Valancourt). Like *Neighbours*, they take place in a
claustrophobic London, masked by fog or darkness, with a sense
of a doom upon it, a city where marked and brooding human
figures encounter shadowy beings who seem to tower over other
mortals by the very reach and intensity of their existence.

Some clues to these novels can be found in his essays in *The
Kingdoms of the Spirit*, published just two years earlier than *Neighbours*. Here he insists upon the spiritual importance of every life:

> each individual life represents a reality of permanent sig-
> nificance and one that is not dissipated by the passing of
> the physical body. It is the belief that each individual life is
> one link in an eternal sequence, that its importance is not
> restricted within the limit of physical duration, that the
> measure of its significance is related to eternity and not to
> time, it is this belief that is the foundation of all the creeds.
> . . . This is the great secret: there is none other. Goethe has
> called it "the open secret".

Like Arthur Machen, Houghton saw this world as the outer husk
of a far greater world beyond. His was convinced that "The Tem-
poral is the shadow of the Eternal". There are various means for
us to gain insights into the rarer realm, including mysticism—in
aspects of all faiths—and literature. But, just as Machen saw a
certain quality as necessary to make true literature—he called
it "ecstasy"—Houghton avers, "Art is spiritual biography, or it
is nothing." And he was sure that some people could access, or

develop, what he called "an added consciousness", though only at great risk to themselves. It was their duty to harness this power, but without losing their essential humanity—he had no time for the idea that such visionaries were superior beings; they were still fully human, and vulnerable. And in his books, where a figure has achieved higher (mystical) powers, it is a matter for humility and care, for these are elusive and potentially perilous: "The soul in each of us is like a seed in that only in silence, in darkness, and in secrecy can it begin its ascent towards perfection."

After about 1940, Houghton's fervour and fierce mystical vision seemed to falter. He was to write eleven more novels, with the last in 1957, but though publishers tried new ways of presenting him, including as a classic crime writer, he must have already looked a somewhat faded and marginal figure. Some of the books certainly have the old spark, and they are always vivid and unusual: no reader could mistake Houghton for a conventional novelist. However, his literary fortunes did not revive before his death in 1961, nor for over thirty years afterwards.

Around about the early 1990s, perhaps, the cognoscenti of recondite literature began to murmur his titles among themselves, and surreptitiously to collect the dusty titles from the gloomiest shelves of vintage fiction. Nothing so strong even as a cult following then, just a stirring of shadows and whispers, aptly enough. But this and the other new editions from Valancourt represent the first surge of recognition for Claude Houghton's original, powerful and mysterious vision for over seventy years. His spiritual archetypes, his demiurges at large in the nightscapes of London, his flawed and restless mortals, have been waiting. We would do well to attend to the strange and sombre testaments they have to tell.

MARK VALENTINE

January 1, 2014

NEIGHBOURS

THE PAST

BOOK I

§ 1

I AM ceasing to live my own life. I see, now that it is too late, how easily one can become so involved in another's life, so absorbed in another's interests and experiences, that gradually one's own life slips into the background, and eventually it becomes merely a shadow. I realize that, for a long time now, my thoughts and actions have not really been mine, but have been only reflections of a strange personality who has dominated me for years. If I attempt to see my own life entirely separated from this personality, I feel that I am nothing but a ghost, and that the man I once was died years ago. In either event, I feel a shadow—either a shadow cast by the living or a shadow cast by the dead.

It is the realization of what has happened to me that impels me to set down a record, however inadequate, of the remarkable events and circumstances that have culminated in such a miraculous manner for me; and although it would appear on the surface that to write such a record should be comparatively easy, it is, in fact, a task of the very greatest difficulty. In the first place, I find it almost impossible to portray clearly the man I was before these events happened to me; and in the second place, the events themselves are so strange in one aspect and so commonplace in another that to represent them accurately would tax the skill of a genius. But I know that I must set down an account of these events, even though it be that only one reader will find therein experiences parallel to his own. . . .

I live in a room at the top of a tall house. It is a fairly large room, and most probably it would be termed an attic, for the walls slope towards the ceiling. It has only one window, and there is that atmosphere of isolation from the rest of the house which is generally associated with attics. Such furniture as there is belongs to me. It consists of a divan-bed, which serves as a couch by day, a table, an easy chair, an ordinary chair, and—books. The walls are lined with them. They even lie in heaps on the floor, having overflowed from the mantelpiece and various cupboards.

But although the furniture is mine, I never intended when I came to this room, years ago, that it should become my home. Quite the contrary. I took it, put my few belongings into it, merely with a view to possessing a refuge in which to mature my plans. I distinctly remember thinking, when I first saw the room, that it would serve for a few months, at the longest, and that then I should have decided on my course, and could go to the environment necessitated by that decision. Had it been prophesied to me that I should remain here for year after year, and that eventually I should lose all desire to live anywhere else, I should have been vastly amused. What innate courage all men possess! With what easy confidence they open a door and cross a threshold! I watch the world from my attic window. I see men and women coming and going, meeting and parting—and I am amazed. So little faith, and yet so much!

I hesitate whether to give the name of the great city in which I live. Better not. It is one of the great cities of the world, but if I give its name I awake in the mind of my reader so many associations, actual or derived, and all so irrelevant to what I have to tell, that they would prove merely distractions. What has happened to me could happen to any one anywhere—it is independent of place or time.

But I must re-create the man who first came here, the man who regarded this attic as a temporary refuge, the man who was myself years ago. No greater indication of my life here need be given than the fact that I find it difficult to remember in any definite perspective the type of man I was when I first came to this attic. What I remember clearly can be stated in a series of brief sentences: I was young; I had a boundless interest in life, and consequently a great enthusiasm; I was very ambitious; I was certain that I should succeed. Those facts I remember very clearly. But if I add one more, I shall complete the list. And the last is this—I remember the nature of the problem that needed solution, and which I came to this attic room in order to solve. It was this:

I felt in myself the possibility of so many careers that I did not know which to adopt. I remember clearly that I used to amuse myself by trying to imagine some activity to which nothing in me responded. It was useless. I had but to imagine a life spent in any surroundings, and immediately something in me seemed to whisper that it could find growth and fulfilment there. And these imaginings were not simply those of a romantic order. I would, for instance, imagine myself as an insignificant clerk, engaged on wholly uninteresting work in a small provincial town, and something in me said that out of the very boredom of such an existence it would derive something unique. It may have been mere arrogance, but whatever the activity or the surroundings imagined might be, there was always something in me which felt confident that it could discover heights or depths which would redeem life from the commonplace. And this "faculty for experience"—as I then termed it—caused me to regard mutually exclusive activities with equal affection. Thus, whereas one thing in me loathed war with a veritable fire of hatred, another thing in me leapt at the idea that it provided the possibility of a comradeship infinitely truer and more real than any of those pallid friendships born of peace—a comradeship tested daily in a living hell of experience. The thing in me that leapt at the possibility of such a comradeship cared nothing for the facts of warfare. It cared nothing for the vast human slaughter created by national hatreds and fears, and accompanied by a huge machinery of lies and misrepresentation even more deadly than the actual weapons employed. It saw merely the possibility of comradeship, and believed that this possibility of individual heaven justified the existence of a general hell. Concurrent with this desire, however, was another which demanded that every energy I possessed should be directed towards the exposure of the false and artificial values which rendered war not only probable but inevitable.

It was the same with everything. I had in me the stuff of a revolutionary and the makings of a reactionary. I could conceive becoming a miner, a pugilist, a preacher, or a politician with equal ease. In myself I found the potentiality of every experience, and if there was that in me which sought to scale the altitudes of all ideals, there was also that which desired to explore the uttermost depths of degradation. I rebelled against the thought that, sooner or later, all this wealth of potentiality would be lost, and that the infinite horizons would narrow until I saw before me the definite and rigid vista of one human life. When this thought came to me, I was literally terrified at the prospect of the magnitude of the surrender, and the narrow limit of the gain. I remember that I used to watch others, and note with amazement their easy acceptance of stereotyped lives—a series of recurring experiences comparable with the revolving cage of the squirrel. I would enter, imaginatively, into these lives, make them mine for an hour, and seek to realize how people supported an existence entirely spent on one well-known level of experience. But always, when I sought to see myself living their lives, I knew that, although outwardly I might force my life to conform with theirs, yet in reality it would not be so. I knew that I would find something above or below the apparent level of their existence which would lend colour to my whole life. Then I would watch others more narrowly, and try to discern some evidence, however small, of a secret life which made their existence possible. But I found little or nothing, and gave it up.

But to be conscious of the possibility of infinite experience is only removed by one stride from experiencing nothing. I had arrived at the stage in which I was so aware of the possibility of adventure in the next street that I saw nothing in the street down which I was walking. What fascinated me was the thought that in one, two, or three minutes I should reach the corner, and that then—well—then anything was possible! But the corner reached, the only choice was another street, and the process continued indefinitely.

What I was seeking was a life into which I could bring the whole of myself. There were many careers open to me, but I knew that, to succeed in any of them, it was essential to concentrate upon and develop merely one part of oneself. "Born a man, died a doctor." It seemed impossible to me. Yet I could conceive of a man who took the whole of himself into being a doctor. I say, I could conceive of such a one; but I knew that the doctors I met might just as easily have been parsons. Every one I met seemed to have had a dip into a bag and pulled out a paper marked "doctor," "solicitor," "nursery-maid," or something, and had accepted the decision. They seemed all right for some, but to me they were ghosts. In becoming something, they had lost so much that, in the end, only a ghost was left haunting a ruin. I used to question people about this, and usually I found that the discussion perturbed them. Also I discovered that practically no one liked what he was doing in the least. Every one wanted to be doing something else. I used to ask people if they loved their work, and they always looked at me as if I were an idiot. "Love it!" one said to me; "good God, no! But you must do something." This remark seemed to me, then, to be an explanation of many things—the faces in the streets, the type of entertainment which was popular, and the general level of the average conversation. What could one expect from a world in which most people disliked their work? Was it any wonder that the faces were loveless, the entertainments vulgar, and conversation a meaningless noise? And I swore that I would not surrender the wealth that I knew was within me for the small change of a narrow career. I registered an oath that I would seek for a life in which I could develop all that I had in me. I would not subject my soul to a series of surgical operations till it was cut, twisted, and at last made to fit some fiddling little occupation or other. To the devil with all that! I was not going to join the army of misfits who posed as the successful. I rebelled against it with my whole being. No! I felt in myself the possibility of a murderer, a saint, a hero, a sensualist, and of every type between these extremes, and I determined that I would seek a life in which all these possibilities should find a means of growth. I swore that I would accept the whole of myself, force life to accept me, and not deny myself out of existence by instalments. And I remember how fiercely I hated all the false modes of self-sacrifice, which were so highly esteemed, by which the young mutilated their lives in order to continue to render possible the existence of the old. Everywhere I saw the young serving that in which they did not believe because of some unhealthy sentimentalism with which they had been drugged from birth. And I knew, then, that if there was one duty in this world, it was to keep one's soul alive, and that this must be done though all mankind condemned one as selfish and inhuman.

Always and ever I saw about me the great unconscious conspiracy to make one sell one's birthright, and I vowed that I would combat it, and that, if I lost my life in the conflict, I could die joyful in the knowledge that I had a life to lose.

§ 2

The paradox is that I ceased to live my own life very shortly after I came to this attic, and yet the life before then does not seem to belong to me at all. I suppose if a man were shipwrecked on a desert island, and remained there year after year, he would find that gradually the details of his old life would seem like incidents depicted in a tapestry—things far off and remote, irrelevant and outworn—and yet his solitary life on the island would, in another way, seem to him to be equally unsubstantial. I suppose my life is something like that. I do not know. But in any event the fact remains that I have now no desire to alter my life, to leave here, or to rid myself for ever of that personality who has gradually usurped my own life in so remarkable and unusual a manner. If I have learnt nothing else from the strange events that have happened to me in this place, I have learnt one thing, and that is sympathy with those who are in any way bound. Yes, it is true. All those who are under the spell of something which they believe to be stronger than themselves are my brothers. I understand them. It matters nothing to me what the particular nature of the fetter may be. I understand the habitual drunkard, the drug-taker, and all the slaves of passion. It is so easy, even for the strong, suddenly to find themselves in the grip of some influence which dominates them and which gradually usurps the very depths of their being. It is easy to term them weak, and to dismiss them. But it takes strength to yield. If the majority do not yield, it is *not* because they have that strength which can overcome, but it is because they do not possess even that lesser strength which dares to yield. I know I am right here. It is the reason why crimes—real crimes—are never committed by nonentities. A nonentity never even commits suicide. A criminal is a strong man gone sour. Any one is strong who dares to make his actions correspond with his desires. It may not be the highest type of strength, but it is strength. People are afraid to recognize this, so they call it weakness. Life is very simple for some people. In fact, life is very simple if you do not live.

Yes, I understand these strong people whom the world calls weak. I can recognize them when I see them in the streets (though I rarely go into the streets now. I scarcely ever go out. I am afraid to leave this room). There is a look in their faces which is unmistakable to one who knows. I have sympathy with them, I pity them, because I understand them. Probably they are the only type I do really understand. And so, you see, I who wanted all experience, I who rejected all activities because of the limitations each imposed, I who wanted to love and understand all humanity, have ended by understanding only those who have ceased to live, because they have become dominated by something which they feel is stronger than themselves! It's very ironical, isn't it? There is a great difference between what we are going to do with life and what, in the end, life does with us. I suppose, before the game begins, the football has its ideas as to what it is going to do with the players. But I do understand these fettered lives, and I know how absurdly irrelevant the advice of well-meaning but ignorant people sounds in their ears. The only help that could reach them would have to come from one who had been held, as they are held, and had freed himself. They would know in an instant if they met such a one—you recognize an old soldier by his scars. This is the reason why I have told no one of my predicament. I do not want to be overwhelmed by the advice of the ignorant. If I meet a man who has had an experience such as mine, I shall know him. There is something in his face which will tell me; and if I see, too, that he has freed himself, I will not let him go until he has told me of the road which leads to freedom. If he would not tell me, I would kill him. But he would tell me—he would not dare to claim such knowledge as his own.

§ 3

Well, that is all I can tell you about the man who originally came here. Whether you find it too much or too little, I cannot help it. So much is necessary and more is impossible. I have told you something of the man, and a little about the problem he had to solve. I have told you that I was that man, and that this is the room to which I came to work out a solution. So the prologue is spoken, the stage is set, and now I have to begin the long drama of what happened to that man here in this room: how he turned from the man I have described into the man who sits here writing, and how the problem which he sought to solve gradually receded until it became as vague as the memory of an indefinite dream. After all, what is the fate of most human problems? They are not solved. Either we grow or we wither, and our problem is either left below us or hovers above us. In either case it becomes irrelevant. . . .

Why is it that to-day is just such a day as that upon which I first encountered that personality who was destined to have so overwhelming an influence upon my life? A useless question. Everything is Chance, or there is no such thing as Chance. But indeed to-day is an exact replica of that day which will live for ever in my memory.

It is dusk, and it is autumn. Dusk is to the day what autumn is to the year, and at this moment there exists a perfect collaboration between the two. It is that hour when dreams seem more real than life, when memories entice more than hopes, when the peace of fulfilment is felt to be more beautiful than the thrill of prophecy. Outside, the swiftly-moving life of the streets grows more and more mysterious as dusk deepens. Lights are lit in houses, shops, vehicles. The voices of the city acquire a strange significance: they are no longer singing the familiar songs of work and pleasure; they are part of a subtle chant wherein the secret of life lurks for the initiated. Everything seems conscious of its own purpose and the relation of that purpose to a whole beyond its guess. Rhythm establishes itself in chaos, and the soul is stirred by the discovery that this rhythm is no sudden innovation, but it exists, always, everywhere, for eyes that can penetrate through the illusion to the heart of reality.

In just such an hour as this I stood in this attic, years ago. I remember that for some time I had gazed out of the window, watching the ever-changing kaleidoscope of life in the streets below, and that a great sense of calm had permeated my spirit.

It was a sense of satisfaction deeper than mere happiness—one of those rare moments when simply to Be is enough; when those thoughts and desires which normally are so insistent in their demands are at peace, lulled by a mystic acquiescence deeper than the source of their own discontent. I remember that I walked about the room, looked at the titles of the books, took down a volume and read a page here and there, replaced it, and renewed again the thread of my meditations. All sense of hurry or the need for decision had left me, and I reviewed lazily the different ways in which I could spend the evening; and I remember clearly that each suggestion that presented itself seemed equally desirable, and that in the very fact that choice was permitted me I felt grateful with a gratitude that was almost joy.

And then—something happened; something so seemingly trivial that even now in retrospect it is well-nigh impossible to believe that it was destined to prove the precursor of events which were not only to transform my life, but eventually to rob me of the sense of my own existence. All that sounds as if that "something" must necessarily have been an extraordinarily dramatic event. It was nothing of the kind. It was merely a laugh on the stairs. No more than that—merely a laugh on the stairs. And yet, as I sit here writing, my hand trembles at the recollection of that autumn dusk of long ago, and all that it meant, and means, to me. Often in life great events have dwarfs for heralds; it is only on the stage that destiny is preceded by pageantry and pomp. In life, a farewell is taken, a door is opened, a laugh is heard—and nothing is ever quite the same again. And yet, did this thing come to me entirely unheralded? Were there not premonitions of a more subtle order than material events? Surely there were, for when I heard that laugh on the stairs, two emotions were simultaneously born within me—one was amazement, the other hatred.

I was utterly amazed. Although I had been in this attic only a few weeks, I had come to regard the top floor of the house as belonging to me. Not that I gave a thought to any other room the top story might contain, as I had no need of it; still, I had that feeling that once I had reached the top of the stairs, one world ended and another world—my world—began. I did remember that there was another room—its door faced the head of the narrow stairs, whereas the entry to mine was to the left—but I had not had the curiosity even to glance into it. I just knew it was there, that I had no need of it, that it was unoccupied, and that, therefore, the top floor belonged to me. I was amazed, and—what was remarkable—I knew instantly that the person on the stairs was not a friend coming up to see me. After all, how easily it might have been! But I knew it was not. I knew it was a stranger, and more, that the person on the stairs had come to live next door. How I knew this with so certain a conviction, I have not the slightest idea. The mechanism by which such knowledge is conveyed is a deep mystery. But all these details about an individual, the only evidence concerning whom was his laugh upon my stairs, established themselves instantly in my consciousness as incontrovertible facts. I knew—and I was amazed. But what, if possible, was even more surprising was that I felt a hatred for this person, whose laugh I had just heard, which surpassed in intensity anything which I had ever experienced. The person who hates at first sight I can understand, but to hate at first hearing is not without originality. I am convinced that the person who did not like Dr. Fell had at least seen him. But, whatever the explanation, I felt arise in me an antagonism against this stranger which was final and absolute. And if any one imagines that I am attributing to our first encounter an emotion which I really experienced later, he is wrong. I know that I felt this hatred then—and immediately. It was not conceived—it was born fully grown. And in that instant I resolved that, if he continued to live there, I would never meet him, never seek to know anything of him—more, that if he remained, I would leave, so determined was I that never in any circumstance would I have anything to do with him.

BOOK II

§ 1

A LAUGH on the stairs—a light, gay, fascinating laugh. A pause. Then a few eager steps, and I heard his voice; evidently he had stopped on the landing outside.

"Come on, Pam. Here we are! This is the top—there aren't any more stairs."

"There couldn't be," a girl's voice answered him. It was rather a deep voice, but gay and attractive. It was the voice of one who laughed much, and the music of laughter was in it. "Oh, good heavens, what a place to choose! Just like you! I shall sit on this stair for a minute to recover."

"Oh, come on up! I want you to see the room. You'll like it. It's just the place I've been looking for."

"What was the name of that book you lent me where the young man carried the young lady up to his room?"

"*Sappho*."

"Well, my dear, you won't be able to do any tricks like that here. It's a pity, because you are so romantic."

"I'm not romantic, Pam. Romance is all nonsense."

"You are, Victor. You're really romantic. All the really romantic people don't think they are. That's why they make such a mess of things."

"You look adorable sitting there."

"I don't feel it. I feel half dead. Why were you so mad on being at the top? That other room you showed me in that other place was all right."

"Oh no, Pam; it was awful. And the woman who owned it was awful too. She had that air of 'I'm-respectable-and-can-prove-it-and-I-hope-you-can-prove-you-are.'"

"Well, who owns this monument?"

"Oh, just a man. A man who clearly cares about nothing except the rent. As long as you pay, you can do as you damn well please.

That's the kind I like. Of course, I'm sorry he's so keen on the rent; but you can't have everything."

"Well, let's see this room of yours. One must be able to see all the world from it. Oh, damn! I've made a ladder in my stocking! It's going to be expensive coming here."

(I heard her run up the remaining stairs, and they entered the room next to mine. I heard the door shut. Should I be able to overhear? I wondered how thick the walls were. Evidently pretty thin, because I heard their voices again quite distinctly.)

"Well?"

"It's all right, Victor. It looks fairly tidy and pretty clean, but of course it won't remain like that with you. Let's have a look at the view. Ugh—roofs, chimney-pots, and smoke. Beastly old town—I loathe it!"

"You don't, Pam."

"I do."

"I love it! It surges with life—activity. My God! how I fought to get here; and now I am here I'm going to use it, live it, get everything out of it that it's got to give. Let's have a look at that ladder in your stocking."

A laugh rang out—a full, rich, young laugh.

"What are you laughing at, Pam?"

"Oh, my dear, you are such a madman! I wonder why I like you? You do know, don't you, that you really are absolutely mad?"

"Why?—because I want to see the ladder in your stocking?"

"But you jump so from what you're going to get out of life here to—stockings! You don't know what you want. You're in a dreadful mess, my dear, and you'll come to a bad end."

She began to sing, and evidently was walking round the room inspecting things. Then she spoke again:

"Who'll make your bed?"

"God knows! There's an old woman comes in, I believe. Least, I think the man—the landlord, you know—said so."

"Oh well! Is there a bathroom?"

"Good Lord! I never asked. Still, it doesn't matter. I can always go out for one."

"You'll forget, for a certainty. I couldn't love you if you didn't wash."

"I'll wash all right. But do you like it?—that's the point—do you like it?"

"Yes; it's all right. It's just the sort of place you would get to. But it's all right. I say!"

"What?"

"Any one else live here?"

(I had been standing motionless, but now I did not even dare to breathe.)

"No; I don't think so."

"But did you ask?"

"Yes—no—I don't know. Damn it, what funny things you want to know! What's it matter?"

"But it does matter, if——"

"Oh yes. I remember. The man said something about some one who was just leaving or had just left. I remember now! I asked him if he was certain the room would be quiet because I worked at night, and he said it would be, except of course for the traffic. Anyway, the walls are thick. Listen!"

He hit the wall, not the one which separated my room from his, but the outside wall.

"Oh well, that sounds all right. But you'd better find out for certain, Victor. Still, it is handy that there's a restaurant on the ground floor."

"But that's the whole idea, Pam. I'm not half such a fool as you think. We needn't come in together, and if any one sees you coming in alone, they'll think you're going to lunch or dine or something."

"And you can still be my secret?"

"I can still be your secret. I tell you, Pam, when we shut that door there, we shut out the whole blasted world! And the best thing to do with it, too!"

"Now you're not going to begin! Promise!"

"No, of course not. But, my God! I am glad that we've got a place where, when we're here together, we can just blot them out—all of them—forget them! Just bang the door on the whole blooming asylum. I tell you, this world is an asylum: those who suffer from the same kind of insanity band themselves together and call themselves sane. I say this——"

"Victor! You promised you wouldn't. What is the good of promising me when you break it directly we are alone? Oh, that blackness in you, that bitterness! That's when I hate you—when you're like that. And you're nearly always like it. You're getting worse."

"I'm not, Pam. I'm not really. I get like it when I'm not with you, and then, when you do come, sometimes, somehow, it all wells up in me. I'd never be like it if I saw you more often. I love the world when I'm with you, but I loathe it when I'm alone—loathe it, my dear: pack of dangerous lunatics! I tell you that when I don't see you I wish to God the whole cursed lot could just be wiped out. Destroyed!—utterly and wholly destroyed! Do you know, if there were a button on that wall, and I knew that if I pressed it the whole world would instantly be blown to smithereens, I'd press it."

"You wouldn't."

"I would! If I didn't, I'd have the responsibility of God, and I wouldn't have that, thank you! But don't let's talk about these things, Pam. We always do when you're here, and then, when you've gone, I feel that I could kill myself for having wasted our time together."

"But I like you to talk—only, I hate you when you're bitter. There's something terrible in you. I can't describe it. It's—black! And when you talk like that, all your face is distorted, and I hate you. You are not you then. You're something else."

Pause.

"I'm all right really, Pam. It's only—I don't know. Don't let's talk about it. Damn everything! We're here together. What else matters? You look marvellous, and I love you. Give me a kiss, and don't let's be serious."

"My dear, no one has ever accused me of wanting to be serious. It's about the only charge that has not been made against me. Now, come and kneel down by the side of me here. There! that's right. Now, smile—more! That's better. Now listen. You may be twenty-three, but you're only a babe really."

"I'm not."

"You are. Don't contradict; it's very rude. Now you've got to give up being bitter. You've got to be happy. You've got to get on with your work and get some money for me—did you speak?"

"No. What I was feeling was too deep for words."

"Well, you must admit that you don't want money, do you? it's no good to you. You always said it wouldn't solve your problem."

"No, it wouldn't."

"Well, it solves all mine. So, you see, it's clear that I ought to have it, and that you ought to get it for me, isn't it?"

"Oh, perfectly. How simple life is for you, Pam."

"It isn't. Life's never simple for a woman."

"Go on! You got that out of a dud play! Besides, you aren't a woman, you're a girl."

"Never mind. And don't start talking about life again. Life's all right, if you leave it alone. It will look after itself. Now what was I talking about?"

"Yourself."

"Yes—and I seldom get the chance with you. Yes, about myself—and money, I remember! Well, you must write, be a good boy, not be bitter, and—oh yes—you mustn't be jealous!"

"I'm not. It's the only emotion of which I am ignorant."

"You're a conceited little beast, but I like you. God knows why—I don't! You mustn't be jealous because, when the new show opens, I can't spend all my time with you."

"Oh, damn the show!"

"Don't be silly, Victor! The show will probably damn itself, and then where shall we be? If it doesn't run, I'll have to go where I can. Do be reasonable! But I can't spend all my time with you. You must work. We must work together—in secret."

"When do your cursed rehearsals start?"

"Next Monday. Why?"

"Oh, then we've got till then. Don't let's bother about anything till then. I say, you might have some free nights during rehearsals, mightn't you?"

"I might. Also I might win that lottery in which I took a bob ticket. Also, you might behave yourself——"

"Shut up, Pam."

"But you will be sensible—you won't be bitter, you will work? Promise! Promise!"

"You've got wonderful legs, Pam."

"Possibly, but that's not the point. You *have* listened to what I've said, haven't you?"

"Look! that ladder has gone all the way up."

"Well, you'd better come down it, rung by rung."

"I think I'll write a sonnet about your stockings and call it 'Jacob's Ladder.'"

"Don't be so absurd, Victor! Whenever you're nice, you're tiresome. And when you're not tiresome, you're black and bitter. I don't know what to do with you."

"But it is all right up here, isn't it? You do like it? I don't know why, but I feel that coming here marks an epoch somehow. I can't really explain what I mean. Directly I saw this room, I felt it. Of course, I've lived in heaps of places, but I only felt I was camping out, so to speak. But here it's different. I'm certain things are going to be different here."

"You mean, all the dreams are coming true and all the ships are coming home."

"My dear Pam, that sounds like a popular song. Listen:

All the dreams are coming true,
    All the ships are coming home;
God has brought me back to you,
    Nevermore apart to roam.

There! that's the sort of tripe that was once popular, and still is. Fortunes are made out of stuff like that. All that's needed is a melody of sugary slush, and the thing's done. Meanwhile geniuses take clerks' jobs because they don't believe in starving any more. What a world! What were we talking about?"

"You—surely."

"No, we weren't. Oh yes, we were!—about this room and my first impressions. Still, that may be all nonsense. What isn't nonsense is that you're here. That is the only fact in the world at the minute that causes me the smallest satisfaction. And listen, Pam—to-night, what about to-night? You're coming here, aren't you? You are coming?"

"I don't know, Victor."

"But why not? What rubbish! Look here: if you're going to start rehearsals on Monday, you are free till then, anyway. You've got to—you must. I want you. Why, it's over a week——"

"Yes, but I've got to be jolly careful. You're so impetuous, Victor."

You think you've only got to want something and it must happen. And if it doesn't, you rave against heaven and earth and the waters under the earth. It never seems to occur to you that I can't keep on staying out all night without the family noticing anything."

"But you can lie, Pam; you've done it heaps of times."

"Yes; but one has to vary the lies, my dear. And that needs imagination and memory—particularly memory."

"But say you're staying with a girl from the show; you can easily do that."

"Yes, and it's been done pretty often. And I have to invent a name for her, a home for her, relations for her, occupations for all of them, and, above all, excellent reasons why my family can never meet any of this crowd of fictions."

"You're wonderful, Pam."

"I'm not, my dear; I'm very human. And I wasn't a liar till I met you."

"Well, it's given you a good memory. Some people pay to get that."

"Yes, Victor; but they only pay in money. It's pretty risky for me, I tell you."

"You'll do it, Pam; promise me you will—tonight. Look here; we can go out to dinner—a better place than the usual one; I've got some money—and then we can come back here. You must, Pam; you must! There'll be a moon to-night, and when we're weary of that we will light a hundred candles."

"Oh, Victor, and you said you weren't romantic!"

"That's not romance—it's a sense of beauty."

"They're the same thing, but you won't admit a sense of beauty if it's smaller than your own. You're an artistic snob."

"I'm not, Pam! It's a fearful lie! But say that you will; say that you will—to-night!"

"Well, if you promise never to be jealous, or bitter, or——"

"Pam, you will! You darling! Come on, let's go now. The sooner we go, the——"

"Now, Victor! you're not going to spoil dinner because——"

"Of course not! Come on, you darling! Quick! Come on! It's easier going down than climbing up. Look, there's the moon. It will be full when we return. . . ."

§ 2

I heard them trip lightly down the stairs. Night had crept into my attic. I stood there alone, in the deepening darkness, but I did not light a candle. I simply stood motionless and tried to establish some sort of order in my conflicting emotions. After all, why was I disturbed? What had all this to do with me? There was nothing unusual about it. And why, above all, did I hate this man Victor? What did he matter to me? But I did hate him with a fierce, unreasoning hatred. So he was a writer, was he? Well, that settled it. I would not solve my problem by becoming a writer. I would never meet him, never know anything of him. I was always quiet in my room. He need never know. As to friends calling—well, there weren't so many, after all, and I could arrange something. Also I'd arrange that he didn't see any light under my door. Yes, I would keep clear of him, and in a few weeks, at latest, I would move, and forget everything about him. Then I began to wonder how the girl—Pam—could really like him. Did she really care about him? Well, to the devil with both of them! A few weeks, and I should be gone, and then I'd never give either of them a thought again.

Still the question recurred in my mind—why was I disturbed? I could find no answer, but gradually I became conscious of the fact that in some utterly fantastic way the presence of the man next door threatened me. Yes, that was the word—threatened. It was absurd, ridiculous; but it was there. I remember thinking, as I stood there, that such an idea could only come to a madman. I felt nervous, alone, wretched. I had no desire to go anywhere or do anything. All the wonders that dusk had stirred in me had vanished. The colours and shapes had departed from things. And then (even now this is a mystery to me) I decided to write down the conversation I had just overheard—or as much of it as I could remember. I think I had the idea that to do this would dispel the absurd notion that it had, or could have, any significance. Still, whatever the reason, I wrote there and then what I could remember, and that is the reason why I have been able to reproduce it in this record. I lit a candle, took paper, and began to write. Very shortly after I had finished making notes on the conversation I had just overheard, they returned. They came gaily up the stairs, chatting and laughing. I immediately extinguished my candle and remained alone in the moonlit room.

§ 3

"There you are! I told you the moon would be full. I say—the room's flooded with it! Wait a minute; I'll draw the curtain right back. There! It's marvellous! I wish God had said, 'Let there be moonlight.' I loathe the day. It's blatant, clear-cut, commonplace. I live for the night, Pam. It's mysterious, subtle——"

"Do stop talking, Victor! How you can go on when you've climbed up all those stairs, I don't know. Lord, you make this room seem like the top of 'the Tower of Babel'!"

"I must talk when I'm with you. I only really talk when we're together."

"Oh, what a lie, Victor! I saw you walking along with a man in the street the other day. I say 'walking,' but really you were hovering over him, talking, talking, talking! His face was green and his eyes were glassy. It's a miracle you weren't run over."

"Oh well, that was Henderson, and he's got a 'sense of peace,' as he calls it, that makes me furious. Take your hat off. I want to see your hair in the moonlight. Why the hell you wear a hat with hair like yours—marvellous blue-black hair——"

"My dear, there isn't such a thing."

"There wasn't till you were born. And a forehead like yours to be hidden! It's all ridiculous! There, that's better! Don't look at me like that or I'll murder you! I almost forgive life when I look at your eyes. The shadow of every mystery went to their making."

"I say, Victor, why did you tip the waiter half a crown? It was much too much."

"Because I've a beautiful nature. Because if one's generous there's no need to be just. Because the thought of you was like fire in my blood. Because the moon was looking on, and because I thought that the poor devil might have a Pam of his own—in which case he'd need all the half-crowns he could get. There—do you want any more reasons?"

"No, no—Heaven forbid! Give me a cigarette—thanks; that's better. Now a match. I say, it's awfully warm up here. Do you think the house is on fire?"

"No, I am. It's a good thing for you it is warm."

"Why?"

"You'll know soon."

"Don't be absurd, Victor. Now talk—only talk sense. I like you to talk when you're sensible."

"Sense! Who the devil wants to talk sense? Common sense has ruined life. What! talk sense when you and the moon are here! My dear, it would be like reading 'Self-Help' in heaven. Pam, I tell you this—the secret of life is to dream. Yes, it is! Always to escape from the hideous, squalid reality. That's the secret. What do we value in the Past? The dreams of the dreamers. They alone live. Common sense has turned earth into a cemetery, and common sense itself lies buried in a million million nameless graves."

"You know, Victor, if you write stuff like that, you can't be surprised if it's not accepted. People like to think they're all right, and that the world's all right too."

"Of course they do! They're dreadfully afraid the nightmare will end. Do you know, Pam, I've a mission in life?"

"I thought you must have something like that."

"Shut up! or I'll put you over my knee and smack you. Yes, I've a mission in life!"

"Well, tell me before you burst."

"My job is to disturb people."

"You are a little beast!"

"To disturb them, Pam. That's the job. First wake them up, then make them doubt, and then make them rebel."

"Ruin their happiness, in other words?"

"Rather! It's not worth much if it can be ruined. I want to knock over all the little card castles that people think are so solid and certain. I want to send their souls out naked into the mystery of things. When you lose the spirit of wonder, you lose everything. That's the job, and I'm going to do it, somehow. I won't fall into line with common sense, I won't conform, I won't say the stones are bread when I know they are stones."

"I'm sure you'll end up in politics."

"In politics! Good God, Pam; I'd rather become a parson!"

"Well, why not, my dear? But they'd never get you out of the pulpit. No! You'll end up in politics."

"It's awful the way people always say to me, 'You'll end up' in so-and-so. Every one is so interested in what you 'end up' in. Now, it's perfectly clear that anything one 'ends up in' can only be a form of death."

"I love you when you say 'it's perfectly clear.' Because, when you say it, it sounds perfectly clear, and I think to myself, 'Well, that's that.' Then I leave you, and I can't remember a single word you have said. Still, I think you're right—you are rather a disturbing person."

"Haven't disturbed you much, anyway."

"Well, I'm not so sure. I think I find everything a bit more difficult since I met you. Where's the ash-tray?"

"Oh, why did you move? You looked a marvellous, untamed creature lying on that couch with your skirt over your knees."

"Hush, Victor! If I read that in a book I should think the heroine was an abandoned woman."

"Yes, it's perfectly true—our simplest, everyday thoughts and acts are quite unprintable. That's why life is so much more interesting than books."

"Whenever you agree with me, I find that you are agreeing with something I didn't say."

"That's because, in my agreement, I establish contact with the implications of your statement."

"Good heavens, Victor! That sounds like a dictionary struck by lightning."

"You're cunning as the devil, Pam."

"Why?"

"You always get me to talk. No—don't move! Kiss me. Again! Harder! There! What shall I do with you? It's queer, but when you are in my arms I never know whether I want to kiss you or murder you."

"Ah, now I do know why that is."

"Why?"

"Because something in you hates me."

"Rubbish!"

"No; it's true."

"It's not, Pam!"

"It is. There's something in you that hates every woman."

"Rot! It's absurd. Whatever makes you think so?"

"I don't know, but it's true. I'm awfully sorry for you, Victor."

"But why?"

"Oh, I don't know. It's difficult for you—it will always be difficult."

"Oh well, I know that."

"No; I can't explain. But I know what I mean. You think you know why it's difficult, but you don't."

"Oh, this is fine! I love you when you talk about me."

"You love every one who talks about you, Victor."

"You'd better be polite, my dear. You will shortly be in such a condition that you will invite a smacking without any other provocation on your part."

"Do be serious, Victor, because I am."

"I am serious, too. I don't hate you. I love you—terribly. Tell me, then, why you think it will be difficult for me."

"I can't really tell you, but, for one thing, the women who care for you won't care for you in the way you care for them. That sounds a bit involved, doesn't it?"

"You're a little devil, but I love you."

"I see you're not going to talk any more. Well, what I said is true, Victor. You'll find it's true."

"I shall find that you are white and round, and that you look like a goddess when your only robe is the moonlight."

"You're so certain that's going to happen, aren't you?"

"Absolutely."

"You do look queer with your mass of hair, your deep-set eyes with their yellow spots round the pupils, and your funny, fierce face with its pointed chin."

"Don't be personal. Take your things off, Pam, all of them, and let the moonlight dance round the flame of your body. I only believe in God when I see you naked."

"I'll go, Victor, if you talk like that! I will really! You say terrible things! You're wicked—yes, you are; don't laugh—you're wicked, and people think you are good. If you say anything like that again, I'll go."

"But it's true, Pam! Your beauty redeems life for me. It lends it a meaning. It justifies all this hell of suffering, squalor, and littleness. I tell you—whether you like it or not—that your body is the only altar at which I can pray. It's true! it's true! Damn it, I don't care—it is true! I love you, worship you, and I hate everything else! I won't let you speak! I'll kiss you so that you can't. There! there! and there! Laugh, Pam! Look at me and laugh! There! You had to laugh, and now we won't be serious any more. We won't, I tell you! You darling!—you're what I've got out of the wreck, and I'm not going to let you go. Do you hear? Never, never! Come, one cigarette, and then your beauty and the moon will make midnight marvellous."

"You really are the maddest creature ever born! Oh, don't, Victor; I can't breathe! Come on, give me that cigarette. It's anyhow a breathing space."

"Here you are. Now that's right. We'll smoke these cigarettes like respectable people clad in the livery of civilization. 'Livery' is the right word—it's the one normally applied to lackeys. Now, are you comfortable?"

"Yes; bring a chair and sit by me and be nice. I'm not sure that I like that moon; it looks as if some one were looking in."

"Oh, it doesn't, Pam. It's a honey-coloured miracle. I can't draw the curtains—yet. I'm going to share your beauty with the moon, just to prove to you that I'm not jealous."

"You are jealous."

"I'm not. At least, not in the way you use the word. I want you to believe in my values. I don't want you to be like all the rest and sell yourself for a bit of tinsel."

"Oh, Victor, you make so many demands on me—physically, mentally, and—oh, I don't know—because I don't follow half you say. Do you know, I've never done a quarter as much for any one else. You make everything that's wrong seem right."

"Rubbish!"

"It isn't rubbish. I do all sorts of things for you that I should have thought were awful once."

"You mean I've educated you."

"The devil of you, Victor, is that you're so nice when you get your own way. You're charming now because you know that I'm going to do what you want."

"You darling!"

"But if I were to refuse, you'd be absolutely beastly. You can be more loathsome than any one I know."

"Well, that's only saying what a fine, rich, full temperament I've got. You're very fortunate in your lover, Pam. You might easily have got hold of a dreary fellow with dank hair, tramping about on large feet."

"I might have got a delightful person with money, who would have done everything I wanted."

"My dear, you'd have died of boredom."

"Lord, how we talk!"

"Yes—isn't it glorious? I feel absolutely happy. I could play marbles with the stars!"

"My cigarette's gone out, Victor."

"That's significant."

"Do you really want me to?"

"Don't be absurd. Of course."

"It may be cold, you know."

"You said how warm it was."

"How irritating you are! Well, if I do, can I finish my cigarette then?"

"You can have another one. I am not a mean man. Take them off, Pam. Take them all off."

"What I've done to deserve this, I don't know. Still, I suppose I've got to."

"That's right. Here, give me your skirt. This cupboard shall be your wardrobe. Good God! you know, it's really ridiculous; you wear simply nothing! Just look at you!"

"Well, I look very nice, don't I?"

"Adorable—but take them off. Here, I'll take them. The moonlight silvers your body. Pam, you look marvellous, terrifying! In your clothes, you're just a girl, but out of them you're a goddess, a mystery. You look like an idol to which the generations of men have prayed in vain. Here, I'll take your stockings off."

"Well, don't ladder the other one."

"You're dreadfully practical, Pam."

"Stockings are dreadfully expensive, my dear. Well, I must say you did that very carefully. Now are you satisfied, you villain?"

"Absolutely. I want a new language in which to describe you. Lie on the couch; the moon has turned it into a silver throne."

"You're a child, my dear. I suppose that's why I put up with you. Can I have that cigarette now?"

"Of course you can. You can have anything you want."

"I am fond of you, Victor, you know—really fond of you, I mean. I've proved that, haven't I?"

"Yes, of course you have. You're a darling, Pam. I'm half afraid of you. You lie there so still and white in the moonlight. Even your voice seems to change. You're Woman—you're Eve. I see your beauty—I remember the wrongs all the ages have inflicted upon you—and I'm half afraid."

"I like the sound of that, but I don't know what it means."

"Directly you are revealed in all your beauty, this half-fearful mood comes upon me. Lying there, like that, you rouse something deep in me—something deeper than desire. I wasn't lying just now when I said that I only believed in God when I saw you naked. You shouldn't have been angry. It's true. And if people think that it's blasphemous or immoral to say that, then they've never worshipped truly at any altar. It's better to worship at the altar of your body than to go to sleep in church."

"You make me believe that that is true, Victor. What a funny child you are!"

"Why?"

"Oh, I don't know. But this isn't exactly the moment when most men would sit there and talk as you are doing. I'm certain you'll have a horrible life!"

"I wish you wouldn't keep saying that—it's most depressing."

"But it's true, Victor. You only think you want things, but you don't really."

"You think I don't want to sleep with you?"

"No, not really, my dear. You're afraid to admit it to yourself because you think life would become a blank."

"That's nonsense, Pam. At least, I hope it's nonsense."

"It isn't, Victor. Do you know, I never gave my body a thought till you praised it. And then I did realize that it was beautiful."

"Then, if I die to-night, my existence is justified! What did I tell you? I said my job was to disturb people. Well, I've disturbed all that commonplace acceptance that you had concerning your body. The result is that you realize that it is beautiful. That's worth a million sermons by men who are afraid of the body."

"Now don't get arrogant, Victor."

"Hurrah! that pleases me! So you realize your beauty, do you? Another star is born in the darkness. I am justified—I have not lived in vain."

"Perhaps not; but you are vain, Victor."

"I'm not. I merely recognize in a cool, sober manner that I possess great qualities."

"You've never recognized anything in a cool, sober manner in the whole of your life—and you never will."

"You seem to know an awful lot about me, Pam. That's not sarcasm. Sometimes I really think you do."

"In some moods I feel that I know everything about you. That's when I feel most sorry for you."

"I say! This is getting a bit dreary. I've always noticed that on those rare occasions when I'm cheerful the person I'm with becomes terribly melancholy."

"You're most tragic when you're happy, Victor."

"Well, I'm damned! And ten minutes ago you made me promise not to be black and bitter."

"You mustn't be either, my dear, but your happiness isn't real. It's a kind of escape. And your bitterness is dreadful. I give you up. I say, Victor, it's getting a bit cold for me."

"Well, I'll shut the window. I've given the moon a straight deal, anyway. Also I'll draw the curtains. There! These curtains are thick. It's pitch black. You've disappeared entirely."

"And you're only a voice in the darkness."

"I'm going to light all the candles I've got when I can find those confounded matches. Curse that chair! Oh, here they are. Ah! there you are again! Thank God for a match! Now for the candles—one, two, three, four——"

"Good heavens, Victor! how many more are you going to light?"

"All I've got. You look beautifully human in the candlelight. The moon made you unearthly. There! that's better. You're not cold?"

"No. But I'll have to get in soon. It must be very late. We were a bit late coming back. What are you thinking about?"

"Oh, I don't know. Something swept over me. Sometimes something happens, and a mysterious instinct in one whispers, 'Note this carefully; you will remember this in the days to be.' I had that feeling suddenly, as I looked at you lying there."

"You're a dreamer, child."

"I'm a man of action, woman—clear-cut, concise, and certain, marching ruthlessly to my objective."

"You want nothing that you possess, Victor. Really you're married to To-day, but you do nothing but flirt with Yesterday and To-morrow."

"Where did you get that from, Pam?"

"Don't be rude. I'm beginning to say just the sort of things that you do—you know, things that seem quite illuminating; but when you've repeated them once or twice they don't seem to mean anything."

"You're an impertinent little devil. If I didn't love you, I'd torture you."

"Well, that's a jolly outlook! Particularly as you don't love me."

"Don't love you! Are you mad?"

"But of course you don't, Victor! How absurd you are! You're far too concerned with yourself to love any one. You haven't time, my dear."

"Well! After all I've done for you!"

"You've done for me, all right. You're a little fiend, and I hate you. You're contented now because, as I lie here like this, you can say to yourself, 'Well, I've got this hour out of life anyhow'! You've practically said as much."

"I don't think I like you much. I've a good mind to go out and leave you alone here all night. Only, I'm afraid you'd steal the valuables."

"We've talked enough nonsense. Look here, I'm going to get in. It's a bit cold."

"Well, jump in. There, that's right. Lord—how you change! Now you look like a little girl in her nice little bed! You're an impossible creature, Pam."

"It's the only explanation for my being here. Oh, do put out some of those candles, Victor! It's like trying to sleep in the middle of a Christmas tree."

"What made you think you were going to sleep? You really do get the most fantastic ideas into your head."

"You'd better get in, Victor. I'm a bit cold, I keep telling you."

"You're a fearful materialist, Pam."

"I'm not. I'm cold."

"Do you know why women always get their own way, Pam?"

"No. Neither do you. Besides, they don't."

"Shut up! I'm going to give you a bit of pure wisdom. Women always get what they want because, at each moment, they always know exactly what they do want. A man never does."

"I never heard such absolute nonsense in my life! A woman never knows what she wants, and some man keeps on telling her that she wants him till the poor wretch believes him. Oh, do get in, and stop talking! For the love of Heaven, stop talking and let's go to sleep!"

"What liars the erotic poets are!"

"All poets are liars, Victor; it's their business. Do get in and let's get warm. Of course you would have a room on the top of a mountain, and then expect your visitors to undress and sit about talking nonsense!"

"All right, I shan't be a minute. It's a damn shame to put these candles out. I say—have a drink?"

"No!"

"Well, don't shout."

"If we drink, you'll start talking again."

"All right. I say, move up, Pam—how the devil do you think I'm going to get in?"

"Well, you are romantic!"

"How can I be romantic with a woman who regards me as a hot-water bottle?"

"I wish you wouldn't call me a woman!"

"Oh well—a girl then!"

"There! Have you enough room now?"

"Too much; much too much."

"You are the most ridiculous idiot, Victor! I say, I believe I'm going to scream with laughter. Will it matter? I don't think I can help it."

"Matter? No! Let's both roar like bulls. Let's both rock with laughter till the rotten old house falls down. It wouldn't take much. This damned house is as rickety as civilization. Don't lie there and shake silently. It's like sleeping with St. Vitus. That's right—laugh! laugh like hell!"

"Some one will hear, Victor. I—can't—stop."

"Hoo-ray! This is fine! I'll be kicked out of here to-morrow."

"Oh, don't shout, Victor. The house feels awfully empty. Is there any one else in it?"

"Only the ghosts."

"I say, it's not haunted, is it?"

"Yes—by the living. They are the only ghosts I'm afraid of."

"There, I feel sober now.—I'm going to sleep."

"I can just hear you, although you are such a vast distance away."

"Well, there! Is that better?"

"You're a darling, Pam."

"I'm much too good to you."

"Much."

"And you don't appreciate it."

"Put your head on my shoulder, Pam."

"But you don't, do you?"

"Give me a kiss. . . . another! I love you! Do you hear?—I love you! I've got the world in my arms, Pam."

"Yes."

"You do love me, don't you?"

"Yes, Victor."

"And you'll come here again, like this, soon?"

"Oh, Victor, it's always the future with you. We're here together now; isn't that enough?"

"Yes. It is enough. I love you."

"I love you."

"To think that I shall wake to find you here in the morning!"

"I say, Victor."

"Yes?"

"You're not always going to give that waiter half a crown, are you?"

"You—are—impossible! I'll kiss you, kiss you, kiss you so that you can't speak. You shall sleep in a flame of kisses. You darling!"

BOOK III

§ 1

I HAVE written nothing in this narrative for many days. There are several reasons for this. I will give some of them. In the first place, it must be clearly understood that all I have written concerning my first encounter with this man Victor was copied from notes made at the time. That, obviously, is the only reason why I am able to recount the foregoing conversation in such detail. Had I not made those notes then, I should have remembered nothing about it. In order to reproduce this first conversation, it was necessary for me to go through piles of manuscript, for, from that autumn evening when I heard his laugh on the stairs until to-day, it has been my custom to record as much as I could remember of what I overheard. You must realize this. You must realize that for perhaps six years now I have been keeping notes of the strange discussions which have taken place in the room next door. This may seem incredible, but it may become clearer later. But realize, at least in part, what this has meant to me, and you will partially understand why I feel that I am ceasing to live my own life, and why I feel like an echo.

It follows, therefore, that to reproduce the foregoing conversation it was necessary for me to go through piles of manuscript. I must confess that it was not, and is not, in any state of order. As I wrote it, I thrust it anywhere, for I was never clear in my mind as to whether I should ever even read it again. Until recently, the idea of attempting to construct out of it some sort of coherent narrative never occurred to me. For this reason, I suppose, I never realized the extent of the manuscript in my possession. But the search necessary to discover the first record I ever wrote concerning this man Victor has forced me to realize what a vast amount I have written during the years I have been here. Now, I understand why my books have overflowed from various cupboards and shelves on to the floor. It was to make room for the ever-growing manuscript concerning my neighbour. Directly I attempted to gather together all I had written, I found that the whole room was full of manuscript. It was unbelievable. It was everywhere. I found odd sheets between my books and in my books; a sheaf on the shelves here, another sheaf in the cupboard there. Sometimes I discovered quite a bulky manuscript which contained a coherent account of discussions and events which were clearly an attempt at a chronological narrative—but it broke off, and the thread was lost. Most often, however, my search revealed merely a few sheets fastened together, in which was recorded some conversation I had overheard. There was no date or any other indication whether the conversation recorded had occurred a year ago or five years ago. Sometimes—often, in fact—I would discover simply a single sheet on which a few sentences were written. Frequently during my search I would pause and read what was written on one or other of these odd sheets, but often what I read seemed entirely meaningless; and, which was peculiar, it did not seem that the sentence recorded was meaningless merely because it lacked a context. On the contrary, I found it impossible to imagine a context, but I was haunted by the conviction that it had a meaning. I know that I cannot make this clear, and that to give examples at this stage would be worse than useless.

This is the chief reason why I have not written in this narrative for many days. I have spent those days in going through the vast collection of miscellaneous notes in my possession. (I will not attempt to indicate what these days have meant to me.) At first it seemed that I must attempt to sort all the scattered manuscripts into some kind of order. This idea presented itself for two reasons: in the first place, I thought that then I should be able to establish some kind of relation between the scattered parts and, in the second place, it seemed that, lacking order of any kind in the material at my disposal, it would be impossible to write this narrative upon which I am now engaged. But I found that the difficulties were insuperable. I could not establish order where all was chaos. Had I been able to detect, in going through all these sheets, any principle of order present in my mind at the time of writing them, I might have been able to arrange the whole manuscript in accordance with that principle. But I found nothing. All I found was a record of a conversation, or a fragment of a conversation—simply a reproduction of something heard. It was so clear in looking over the sheets that I had simply written down what I had heard, and then put my record into some receptacle and forgotten everything about it. Yes—forgotten. During the many days I have just spent turning over and reading parts of this scattered manuscript, I was amazed again and again to discover that what I read represented something that had passed entirely from my memory. I believe it is true to say that, if I had not preserved at the time a record of the conversations I had overheard, I should not now be able to recall a single one of them. I suppose it is partly this fact which has made these last days so painful. And as I read a sheet or two here, or dipped into a bulkier manuscript there, I felt the impossibility of the narrative upon which I am now engaged. How could I attempt to write a record of what has occurred to me in this room, when the only material for such a task was a chaos of manuscript? This question presented itself to me again and again during the past few weeks, and a hundred times I have been on the point of destroying every word of what I have written here and giving up the task as hopeless. And yet something deeper than reason urges me to go on and to attempt the impossible, so I have decided to continue—for although it is pain to write, I feel that I must obey the urge within me, and attempt to construct a narrative out of my experiences in this room, although I know that such a narrative must of necessity be pitifully inadequate.

So I have returned to my desk. I sit here writing in this attic of mine. All around me, in a state of complete confusion, lie the sheets of a vast manuscript upon which I must draw for almost every word that I write here. On all of it the dust of the dead years lies thick. I sit here calling the dead to life. I try to believe that some instinct will guide me in my selection, and that by its aid I may light upon the significant in what lies around me and reject the irrelevant. That is the faith that comes to me in my best moments. In others, however, I feel that the very sheet I am writing now will but fall from my desk, as each of those around me has fallen from it in its day, and will become but another withered leaf amid the relics of the great autumn that surrounds me.

But even so, what else remains for me to do? I have said that I am ceasing to live my own life; it would have been truer to have said that my life is over. Well, in justice to myself—in justice to what I once felt myself to be—I must attempt to record the events that have brought me to this. A man rarely commits suicide without leaving a written reason for his act. I must, and I will, attempt to record—for myself—how another personality has taken possession of my life, until it seems that I have ceased to live except through him. I will set it down here. After all, none but I will know how utterly and hopelessly inadequate it is.

§ 2

I know that in writing this narrative it will be necessary for me frequently to interrupt, otherwise this work would be nothing but a series of conversations. But there is one thing that I will state here, for it is necessary to emphasize it. I have never seen this man Victor, who has effected such a revolution in my life. If I have been false to every other vow, I have been true to that one I made when I first heard his laugh on the stairs. I vowed then that I would never see him, and I have been faithful to that vow.

From that autumn dusk to this moment in which I am writing this page, I have never set eyes on him. And how many years is that, I wonder?—six, ten, twelve, fifteen? I do not know. Only organized lives have need of time. No, I have never seen him. Does that seem strange? Does it seem impossible to you that two men could live in adjoining rooms and never meet? It will not seem peculiar to you if you have ever really exercised your will and, therefore, know what it is capable of accomplishing. I assure you that to remain unknown to this man Victor was an easy task. Very soon I became aware of his movements, and before very long I seldom left my room. And even then I only went out at night. Food never attracted me greatly, and my needs soon became those of a hermit. No, I have never seen him, for from the first I hated him, and this hatred grew in intensity. I willed never to see him.

But if this seems incredibly fantastic to you, let me assure you of this: nothing ever imagined, nothing ever written in books, nothing ever dreamed even by a madman, is nearly as fantastic as life itself.

If you find the imaginings of men to be strange, eerie, divorced from sober reality, and life itself to be clear-cut, definite, and solid, then I assure you that you know nothing about the nature of life. What actually happens in life itself is so incredible that men do not dare to believe it, and so they accept it by the simple process of terming all the miracles of existence the "commonplace." If a man arises to tell them the facts concerning the commonplace, they retaliate by calling him a poet. It is only the dreams that visit men by night that they call fantastic, but that infinitely greater dream which visits them day by day they regard as the solid and familiar countenance of the real. I suppose some instinct prompts them not to disturb the surface of things. Question anything, and soon you will question everything.

It is true. And if men are forced to recognize in certain moments the mystery that surrounds them, they swiftly devise a short-cut to certainty. "Are there mysteries?" they say. "Well, death will reveal everything. We have only to die to know all." Ah, these practical people!—they are the real dreamers, did they but know it. They imagine that death will solve everything. And I suppose, in some dim spirit-world where once they awaited birth, they argued that they had only to be born in order to be initiated into all the mysteries.

But why speculate about all this? If you, whoever you are, find my narrative a fantastic one, I ask you to search out your own life, recall all that you can remember from the date of your birth until now; review in retrospect all the hopes, desires, dreams, and passions that have been yours or still are; reflect upon the passage of your life, and see yourself—as you are in truth—a living soul upon a speck of dust whirling through an infinity of space, and then ask yourself whether anything remotely approaches in phantasy the incredible and amazing dream of your own existence?

§ 3

I had been asleep, and the sound of voices suddenly wakened me.

"Hullo! By Jove, it's you, Tim! Come in man! Don't stand peering at the place as if you'd discovered me in an asylum."

"So this is where you've hidden yourself. You're a queer fellow,

Victor. I say, what a climb! Well, how are you, anyway?"

"All right. Sit down. I'm glad you came. I'm fed up with everything."

"I heard you'd a love affair on; is that right?"

"Of course. I've always a love affair on."

"What's she like?"

"All right. Of course we have rows."

"Naturally. Well—you don't mind my putting my feet on the table? Good! Well, I'm pretty up against it. This world seems to think it can get on without me."

"I know—the world is curiously blind. It thinks it can get on without me, too."

"Ah well, that's different. You're a dreamer, Victor. You write verse. You've told the world to go to hell right from the beginning. You can't complain if it cuts you dead. But it's different with me. I'm practical. I'm a scientist. It can't get on without me."

"Sheer egotism!—and mostly lies!"

"No, it's true. Look here. I want to talk with you. I don't know what the hell to do. You see, my trouble is I'm not *simply* a scientist. I don't want to see life always through a laboratory window. To succeed as a pure scientist, you have to be narrow. In this sense you've got to be satisfied wholly with abstract thought."

"And you can't sleep with abstract thought."

"Shut up, Victor! I'm serious. I've a good mind to chuck everything and go in for journalism. I say, is that a photograph of your love affair? She's on the stage, I suppose? She's got damned good legs."

"I'll tell her you said so. Well, go on. I thought the higher sciences were above legs. What are you going to do, really?"

"Isn't it a putrid little world, Victor? No, but really? Aren't they all a crawling, miserable, little lot of swine? Ugh! Damn it, just think what interests them! Do you know, I think there's as much difference between one man and another as there is between an elephant and a mouse. It's a difference of kind, that's what I mean. Compare Beethoven with some overfed swine just reeling out of one of those cursed restaurants. It's absurd to call them both men."

"Don't stop, Tim; go on. I love it when you become a revolutionary."

"Well, I don't care; I think the whole damned thing will crash, and I don't give a damn if it does. Do you care? Do you give a damn for it?—it doesn't give one for you."

"Oh, let 'em do what they like, Tim. At the very best they've only learnt how to die. If any one tries to tell them how to live, they crucify him on some cross or other."

"Well, there you are! Suppose I go on at this science of mine— pure science, I mean—what happens? Some mug, comparatively speaking, applies it, as they call it—gets the credit of the whole thing, and what takes place? Either they learn to kill each other in enormous numbers in a hitherto unbelievable way, or some swine of a financier is enabled to flash his filthy orders more quickly all over the world. What a triumph for pure science! All we scientists do is to give dangerous weapons to lunatics. But even the scientists are such bloody fools that they don't see it."

"You're right enough. Man's not fit to possess power."

"Well, he's got power all right. And he'll soon have power at his command such as he's never dreamed of. After all, it's not nonsense to say that soon they may have power enough to blow the whole confounded planet to smithereens. And it's the result of the work of a few hundreds of men. Do you know that, if it hadn't been for the work of a handful of men in each age, mankind—if it had survived—would still be living in caves?"

"Well, they still are, mentally. Don't talk to me about your damned science! I don't know anything whatever about it, and I don't want to. But I'll tell you the man who is the world's biggest fool, bar none, and that's the man who thinks science will save the world. Shut up! don't speak—I'm going on! I saw an article by a great scientist the other day, and what do you think his view is? It's this. That everything will be all right soon, because science will do all the work, produce all the food, and so on, and that—then— men will have leisure. Leisure! I ask you—does the poor fool really think that people want leisure?"

"Well, I do."

"You think you do, Tim, and you may. I doubt it, but I'll give you the benefit of the doubt. You might just manage with your mathematics, plus legs in silk stockings. (I suppose science will turn out silk stockings all right?) But think of the majority of men—if they had leisure! By God! it's the one thing they're afraid of. They flee from it like the plague. If you've leisure, you are forced to think. Well, that takes courage—much greater courage than to die in a trench. It takes much more courage to live than to die, but it's easier to die, so it's always been the fashion to call it bravery. Leisure for the race! Why, there's no one will spend an hour alone if he can possibly avoid it. But this fool who wrote the article thought they'd be all right if they had nothing to do. They would then, he said, appreciate the arts, and become philosophers. Rubbish! The world would become even a bigger brothel than it is now—if that's possible."

"Well, that's a nice little speech! You're a wonderful lad, Victor. Who was your scientist friend?"

"Oh, I don't know or care. He may have a forehead as high as a house, and he may know all the science that has ever disproved itself, but the fact remains that he is, fundamentally, a dismal and ignorant fool. To hell with him, anyway!"

"Of course there easily could be leisure now. We've machinery enough, but instead of its being our slave we've become slaves to it. But what's the good of talking? I always begin about myself, and in five minutes I'm discussing humanity. Damn humanity! One's got to realize things once for all—most people are fools: they always were and they always will be."

"Right! What are you going to do?"

"I think I'll chuck this science business and write. There's much less competition in the writing game, Victor, and more money. All sorts of complete idiots do quite well at writing."

"Yes—that's their qualification. But how will you get on? You're a misfit, Tim."

"Well, what about you? You get enough to live on by doing nothing in an office and, for the rest, you write just exactly what you want to, and now and again get half a guinea or a guinea for it. Are you going on like that all your life?"

"I don't know what the hell I'll do. I swing between the heights of enthusiasm and the depths of boredom. It seems to me, Tim, that if one really thinks about anything, it soon becomes clear that it's not worth while."

"I don't know—life offers a good deal."

"Yes. And most of it you don't want, and the rest is too damned dear at the price."

"Your trouble is that you want to find a justification for life—a meaning for it."

"Perhaps. I don't know. I suppose until you've got one, everything must be pretty meaningless."

"Oh well, why bother? Perhaps we'll each write a great book some day."

"Well, suppose we do. That's easy enough to imagine. Suppose the mighty works you suggest are written, are lying on that table, are by us, are recognized—well, what then? Even imagine the incredible event that they brought us a lot of money. Still—what then? We could travel, go to expensive restaurants, waste money, and still I say—what then?"

"Oh well, that argument only comes to this—that nothing is worth while, as we've got to die sometime. Well, so we have, I agree; but the point is that we might get a good time first."

"A good time! That's the modern gospel! You and I having a good time would make a good film. I'd love to see you having a good time! Bah! I'm ten times as fed up as you are! Listen! there's some one coming up!"

"Oh, that's Dan. He's back. I saw him at dinner and told him I was coming here. He's the bird for us. No problems about Dan."

"No, you're right, Tim. He's very jolly and excessively depressing. Come in, Dan! I've just said you're depressing."

"Good Lord, these stairs are depressing. Hullo, Victor! There's Tim with his feet on the table, talking. Well, how are you?"

"All right. Tim's only just said you were back. Well, how did you find Europe?"

"Well, the only place where the people are happy is Spain. This first-rate-Power business is all nonsense. You should note the faces of the first-class-Power people. They look like the annual outing of a Suicide Club. But the fifth-rate-Power people sing and dance and enjoy themselves. I'm all for the fall of Empires."

"Victor's been on his usual theme, Dan—fed up and nothing worth while."

"My God, how you two talk and bother yourselves! Why you care a curse about half the things you talk about I don't know. The more I see, the less I care. I don't care a rap about what happens. I paint, I enjoy myself, and if the world goes to hell to-morrow, let it."

"You can't live like that."

"I can, Victor; *you* can't."

"Why bother to paint if the world is going to hell?"

"Because it amuses me. I see what it is: you're determined to talk about God. Well, I don't mind, but if we do, I must have a drink. Come on, let's go out and get a drink and talk about God. You'll come, Victor, for the sake of the conversation, and Tim will come for the sake of the drink. So we're all satisfied. I wish I hadn't climbed all those stairs for nothing. Come on! If you fellows would only really drink, you'd have no problems."

"That's the capitalist creed concerning the working classes."

"Well, they are probably right. They've tried it and ought to know. Come on; with a few mixed drinks we'll create a God of some kind to suit you, Victor. We'll create him to-night, and forget him to-morrow. Is that your latest girl up there? She's all right —make a good model. You must tell me about her. Now, I met a woman in Spain who really was a bit out of the ordinary. . . ."

§ 4

I never understood why people kept diaries, but I understand now. It's not because of the actual happenings recorded in them. Unconsciously, a man who keeps a diary writes for posterity—but it is his own posterity. When he looks over his diary, the events there stated are enough to enable his mind to collaborate with them in a re-creation of the actual atmosphere of the past. As he reads, a whole hour, or one whole day, is born again. But only for him. Another would but find a record of commonplace events. That's why diaries are so uninteresting to the outsider.

So it is with me as I dip into the manuscript which surrounds me. I have just written, in the last section, a fragment of a conversation overheard probably some years ago. To you it may seem merely the rather wild talk of three young men, but, in my mind, every word of it is associated with a winter's night of sudden rain and blustering wind. Till I chanced on the sheets containing that conversation, I remembered nothing of that winter's night, or indeed of the conversation itself; but as I read it over, it all lived for me again and I suffered it all again.

Nothing dies—it only sleeps. Disturb the deep tarn of memory, and misty wraiths of the past will arise before you. Dwell upon them, and they will become substantial. A dead jest will make you smile, a dead sorrow will claim another tear. It is not what I read when I look through my manuscript which disturbs me, it is what it suggests and awakens in my mind. And, in truth, the conversation which I have just set before you brings again to me the whole night of which it formed a fragment. I live again through the depression that had overtaken me as I climbed to this attic at dusk; the terrible indecision as to what I should do with the hours which confronted me; the determination to sleep and so escape; and then the sudden sound of voices, the conversation, and the steps of the three men as they went downstairs. And then—the silence, the blank emptiness! And the shrill, recurring sob of the wailing wind seemed as the moan of a spirit in prison, and the great drops of winter rain were tears falling through the darkness.

§ 5

"Pam!"

"Too late, Victor, my dear; I saw you first! Yes, I saw you before you had time to alter."

"Oh, Pam, thank God you've come! Why didn't you tell me you were coming? I might have been out. How have you managed to get here? I believe you could get here much more often than you do. Have you ever been before when I've been out? It would be just like you to say nothing. I believe you came to spy on me, did——"

"Oh, stop, stop, stop! It's like being in a gramophone factory when they're testing all the records at the same time. Now, do listen for once. I've got half an hour, that's all. I thought I'd give it to you."

"I'll wear it all the rest of the day like a marvellous flower in my buttonhole. And to-morrow I will place it reverently in the garden of my memory."

"Oh, Victor, and you say you're not romantic!"

"Don't argue, Pam. Come and sit on my knee, and tell me if you've been a good girl."

"I can't sit on your knee for a whole half-hour. Still, I will, to begin with. There! Also I'll kiss you—which you don't deserve. There! Now you've got to tell me something, and you've got to speak the truth."

"I always speak the truth, Pam. It's my ruin."

"Hush! Be serious! Oh but, first, do you know I've a solo dance in the new show?"

"I bet you're damned good in it, too."

"I notice you never come to see any show I'm in. That's very unpleasant of you. You ought to want to see me. I look extremely nice in a very cute, though somewhat short, dress."

"I prefer a private view to a public exhibition, Pam."

"You're vulgar, and I hate you. If you really loved me, you'd glory in me. But you don't—you love only yourself and your own horrid, gloomy ideas. And the day you could do without me, you'd throw me away; and if any one ever mentioned me, you'd say: 'Pam? Oh yes, I remember her; rather a pretty little thing, wasn't she? But very shallow, of course. Now, my view is . . .' Victor, don't—that hurt! You're not to pinch me. Besides, you've got to behave properly."

"You know, Pam, some one will murder you one day. I expect I shall, when I've time. And when I'm in the dock, and they ask me to plead 'Guilty' or 'Not guilty,' I shall say 'Neither. I did not kill a woman; I destroyed a principle.' That's what I shall say."

"They'd understand you as little as I do. But I don't want to listen to you, I want you to listen to me. It's very good for you to listen, you know. Isn't it?"

"Sometimes. Very rarely—unfortunately. This may be an exception. Go on, Pam."

"Well, I've been thinking about you."

"You're becoming one of the intelligentsia."

"Shut up, and don't use foreign words."

"Right!"

"Yes; I've been thinking about you, and have come to the final conclusion that you're all wrong and will have to alter."

"Go on, Pam; it's a good opening."

"In the first place, you don't look well. In the next place, you're beginning to stoop dreadfully; in the third place, your clothes are awful——"

"Hurry up, Pam! Get to the end of the Road to Ruin."

"That's just what I don't want you to do. Another thing is, that I really hate one side of you, and if it develops I'll never see you again. Oh, and something else——"

"I can't listen much longer. It's physical pain for me to keep silent when I'm with you."

"You've got to listen. Now, do you know, that when I flashed in through that door you were sitting here looking the picture of misery."

"That's because you weren't here, Pam."

"That's not true, Victor, is it? . . . Is it?"

"No, it's not true, Pam. At least, it's not wholly true."

"It isn't true at all. You were looking as if the end of the world had come."

"Between ourselves, I believe it has. Really, I'm certain it has. My view is——"

"Oh, Lord! Your view is—— Don't go on!"

"You're awfully pretty, Pam, to-day. I like those purple grapes on your hat. Besides, you look like Joy itself. Give me a kiss, and tell me when I'm going to see you again."

"Oh, Victor, whenever I'm with you we spend the whole time arranging the next meeting. Let me get up: I'm too heavy."

"You're an angel from heaven."

"I'm not; I'm a chorus girl. At least, I was until I got this solo dance."

"That doesn't prevent you from being an angel in heaven. There are many mansions, you know."

"Don't talk about heaven, Victor. I'm sure you know nothing about it. Now, tell me why were you sitting here looking like a funeral when I came in?"

"I don't know, Pam."

"You must know, Victor."

"I don't, I tell you. Really, I don't know."

"But you were miserable?"

"Yes."

"And you often are?"

"Oh yes, Pam, often—damn it! Don't cross-examine me. You know we are wasting your half-hour."

"We're not. What is the matter with you, Victor? It worries me. Because I am fond of you, my dear. And I hate to see you unhappy and throwing your life away. I believe you talk all sorts of things that do you no good when you're with your men friends."

"Curse my friends! I hate them all, really."

"You're awfully like a naughty little boy at times."

"Shut up, Pam! We're discussing a Soul's Tragedy. Do let us be as serious as the subject-matter demands."

"No, you're not going to joke me out of it. That's a trick you've got. You're full of tricks. You're as cunning as the devil."

"I'm not nearly so successful."

"Oh, don't joke, Victor! Why do you pretend to be gay and happy when I'm here?"

"Because I am—when you're here."

"It's not real, or else you'd be all right when I'm away. Tell me what's wrong with you—why not?"

"It's not too easy to describe, Pam; and the worst of it is, that when I try to reduce it to words, it all sounds ridiculous, or pretentious, or a pose, or something futile. Some things lose their essential quality directly they are stated. But why the devil should we waste our time like this? I'm happier when I'm with you than at any other time, and I grudge every minute we waste. God knows how long you'll stand for seeing me, anyhow!"

"But I like seeing you, Victor. I only couldn't see you if that thing in you which I hate grew and grew until you became it. You're a child, really. Your head's in a muddle, that's all. You read too much and talk too much, and discuss all sorts of rubbish with people who don't care twopence about you, yourself, but like you because you're vital and they're not. You've surrounded yourself with vamps, my dear."

"You're the only vamp, Pam—'Pam, the Vamp.' It sounds like the title of a film."

"I'm not. How dare you? I was a nice, pure, innocent girl till I met you."

"There used to be a popular song on that inspiring theme."

"Shut up, Victor! I was. You seduced me. You're a bad man. I'm not a pure girl any more. I'm what is called a wanton. I looked the word 'wanton' up in a dictionary last week to see what it was, and I found I was it. I'm not looking up anything else in a dictionary. I don't think it's a nice book."

"You talk more rubbish in half an hour than any one else I've ever met."

"Good Lord! half an hour! That reminds me; I shall have to go. Listen! Will you tell me one day what it really is that makes you such a wretched sort of person, when really you've a capacity for joy far greater than most people?"

"I might, Pam, if——"

"If what?"

"If you come here again soon."

"Now what can that have to do with it?"

"I find it much easier to talk about my soul when I can see your body."

"Oh, what nonsense you talk! We can't always be together, Victor."

"My dear, one must do one's best in this world, and then one will have no regrets. I merely ask you to do your best."

"You're impossible, but you're nice again now. You look different. Your eyes are laughing. You're really rather attractive when you're happy. I think I do love you a little. I might even come here again soon, if——"

"When, Pam—when?"

"If you'll tell me everything, I might come on Saturday."

"You are an archangel, Pam."

"What's the difference between an angel and an archangel, Victor?"

"An angel is in the chorus, whereas an archangel has a solo dance and comes on Saturday."

"Idiot! I must go!"

"Darling!—on Saturday."

§ 6

Remember that I have nothing to aid me in writing the most difficult part of this narrative. All that I have at my disposal is a partial record of past conversations and events, but nothing to indicate their effect at the time, or to show the stages through which I passed before I became conscious of the fact that I was ceasing to be myself. Was it a gradual process, or was the fact quickly established, and only the realization of it that was slow? I do not know. But I believe it was gradual. When the knowledge of the existence of this man Victor first came into my life, I believe that I was only conscious of my hatred for him. And, as I have said before, I know that I felt that he threatened my existence. The world seemed too small for the two of us, and I felt that, in some utterly inexplicable manner, the solution of his problem—whatever that problem might be—would affect the whole of my destiny. If this sounds absurd, impossible, then—if you continue to read—you must assume that you are reading a document written by a madman.

And in truth you may well be right. I have dwelt alone so long, I have been so absorbed with thoughts that appear never to occupy the attention of other men, that it may easily be true that I am not only mad now, but that I have been mad for years. But, remember, that even madness is a part of life, that it has its place and needs its explanation, and that the only definition of a sane man is that he is not mad. Was it not said, when asylums were first being erected, that it had been decided to shut up the mad people in order to give those who remained free the illusion that they were sane?

I do know, however, that my interest in this man Victor was awakened from the very first. The fact that I hated him proved that. (Hatred, or love for that matter, is a sign of consuming interest. The former is a fierce desire to destroy, and the latter is a fierce desire to serve.) I believe, though I am far from certain, that from our first encounter I felt a relief in being able to transfer my thoughts from myself to him. I know that I soon began to await his step on the stairs with an impatience that I should have found difficult to explain. I was eager for the sound of his voice, and—yes, I remember—my original reason for making notes of the discussions I overheard was that, if I failed to do this, I could only remember *his* contribution to the conversation. What was said by his friends, or the girl Pam, I forgot immediately. But the one fundamental fact of which I am certain was that his coming to the room next to mine was destined to affect my whole life. How true this was I have only realized since, but that it *was* true I felt from the beginning. The most remarkable fact of all, however, was that I had no desire to see him, and I have none now. It may well be that I have seen him in the street. I may have passed him as I went through the restaurant on the ground floor of this house, and merely thought that he was some one coming in to dine. Do we ever see the actual form of that which influences us most? I wonder. What importance we attach to that which we can touch and see, and yet the Thought and the Will from which all our actions proceed are both invisible!

I want you to realize that, as I sit here attempting the impossible task of narrating something of that which has happened to me in this room, I am like a man who is trying to write four acts of a play while he is living the fifth. No curtain has rung down on my drama. As I sit here writing, this man Victor is next door. He is alone, and he is walking up and down his room—a habit that has grown upon him much of late. He walks up and down, hour after hour, and often he talks to himself. Often I cannot understand what he says. For some months now he has talked aloud when he is alone. Sometimes I listen, but often I am afraid to listen. I am afraid to stay in this room, and afraid to leave it. The world outside has become impossible for me. It's strange, isn't it? for, after all, it is the same world concerning which, when I first came here, I used to speculate so much. Then, each of its infinite roads seemed an invitation to me, and—now—there is no highway through it down which I can walk. Ah, how rich, warm, and inviting it once was! And how beautiful! My God, the beauty of earth then! I cannot believe that another ever loved earth as once I loved it. I loved it with a passion that bordered on ecstasy, and I swear that, when I first came to this room, I have often lain on my couch at night and heard the deathless song of the stars and known the joy of all the rivers of earth as they flowed towards the sea.

I have been robbed, cheated! The earth is as lost to me as if I had died. I tell you I cannot see that beauty as once I saw it! I cannot feel that love for earth which once made all earth heaven for me! It has all become as an unsubstantial dream! I live another's life, I am a shadow, an echo. I hated him then, and I hate him now. If ever I see him, it will be because I have determined to kill him. No man was ever robbed as I have been robbed. I am the first ghost to write his memoirs.

Yes, as I write, all the time he is walking up and down, muttering to himself; sometimes talking aloud, sometimes laughing. It frightens me to hear him laugh. And why is he so often alone? I can scarcely remember when I last heard any one with him. But I must leave the Present—my concern here is with the Past. I believe that it was to escape from the horror of the Present that I determined to narrate the Past. How we lie! What liars we all are! We set down motives and ascribe causes—lies! all of it. We posture and pretend, even to ourselves. But, anyway, one thing is true: I have realized my own falsity. That's something. I know my own nakedness. One world has come to an end.

§ 7

The more I refer to the manuscript which surrounds me, the more I find myself regarding it as my diary. It is ironical that one's diary should consist of the conversations of a stranger, but this fact is only another indication that I have merely haunted this world and not lived in it. What they will make of me in the next world I really don't know. And it really doesn't matter very much, because I am convinced that I, personally, shall be very much more at home there than I am here. Here, indeed, I was never at home. For one reason, I could never accept what others accepted as being normal and natural. The spectacle of life awoke a flame of rebellion in me, and so great was the intensity of this revolt that I was certain, in the very depths of me, that something was going to happen. What this "something" was I could not have expressed, but I knew that it would destroy for ever the sense of security which people round me possessed, and which seemed to me to be derived from a belief in things not only less than themselves, but outside themselves.

Anyhow, it is very easy not to be at home in this world. To be at home here it is necessary to be hypnotized by the illusions which hold the majority. One thinks that one lives more fully if one has a great zest for life, or a great faith in it, and, in truth, one does live more fully—but it is not the life of this world. To see more it is necessary to be solitary. The valleys of life are only outspread before you if you climb the mountain. . . .

It was a day in early spring—one of those days when the first hint of resurrection comes from the great sepulchre of winter—a day of whispered promise. Beautiful with a beauty beyond expression is the coming of Spring in meadow and woodland, but even more beautiful to me is her unexpected caress in the stony labyrinth of a great city. There she greets one in the midst of that which has denied her, and her beauty is framed in tragedy and illuminated by the halo of pity. In the solitude of the country, she is a goddess: in the loneliness of the city, she is an angel.

Just such a day it was—a day of sudden, bittersweet remembrance, in which, ever and again, a soft fragrance in the air awoke not only exquisite anticipations of a summer to be, but also memories of a vanished spring when one was a child, and all life a garden, made mysterious by the ever-changing shadows of passing dreams. And yet is any day really more marvellous than another? Is it not rather that only on certain days one sees the miracle?

I remember that all the morning I had been out, wandering from street to street, glad that spring had come again, and that, in the late afternoon, I had returned to this room, promising myself an hour of reverie while I rested on the couch. But I had returned only a few minutes when I heard Victor's voice on the stairs and the footsteps of another man following him. . . .

"One can only talk in a room, Hen. And the smaller the room, the better."

"All right, Victor; I don't mind coming up."

"Here we are! Sit down and I'll make some tea. By Jove! it's great to have you here again."

"I always like this room of yours, Victor. It's like you."

"Well, it suits me. I'm glad you like it, though."

"Why?"

"I like you to approve. I don't know why. But I feel more certain about anything if you approve of it. God knows why, because we don't agree about anything!"

"We do—about some things."

"Very few, Hen, very few—and a damned good job for you. I wouldn't want my worst enemy to agree with me. If any one says to me (which he never does!), 'I quite agree with you,' then I know that he is in hell."

"Two things are constant in you, Victor—your egotism and your romanticism."

"I explained to you that I'm not really an egotist——"

"Hush! don't remind me of that!"

"And I'm not romantic either."

"Make the tea, Victor, there's a good fellow. And let's have just a little pleasant small-talk to-day. No themes, no great discussions, no ideas! Just a pleasant afternoon together."

"Impossible, Hen! I want to ask some things most particularly. Damn chatter! I hate it."

"You're wrong. Do you know, you don't *know* anybody."

"What the devil do you mean?"

"What I say. You corner your friends and acquaintances, and simply talk with them in order to find out what they think on those subjects which interest you. It's inhuman. You never get to know any one. Just think! how little of a person is represented by his ideas on subjects which interest you! Scarcely anything—not a hundredth part of the person. Still, you make them do it, then let them out of the corner, and they go away and you forget every word they've said, or you concoct a theory as to why they said it. You've an infectious mental enthusiasm, and that's why people fall into your traps."

"Lord, Hen, what a speech! I don't believe a word of it. I try to discover—always—what it is in a person which enables him to go on at all."

"And how many people, do you suppose, can tell you that? Half of them don't know what you are talking about, and the other half don't care. *You* may live in and through ideas, but other people don't. They don't know what an idea is. You know nothing whatever about human beings, Victor. You're too inhuman, but the devil of it is that people think you're more human than they are."

"Here's your tea. I gather that you don't approve of me, Hen."

"You're tying yourself up into knots which are more easy to tie than undo. I know, because I did something of the same sort of thing once."

"Ah, but that was before you got a sense of peace!"

"There you are! There's an example of what I mean. I once used a stupid phrase in an unguarded moment. I said I had 'a sense of peace.' Well, you fastened on that luckless phrase. You thought, 'I must find out what's behind that.' That's to say, you haven't a sense of peace, and you're determined to satisfy yourself that I'm deluding myself. So you are going to have it out with me. Well, I don't mind. But you're wrong—the method is wrong. Ideas are drugs to you, and you mistake them for life. By the way, how is Pam?"

"Pam? Why on earth did you bring her in? Pam is all right. But directly one gets to know people they become so confoundedly mysterious. When I first knew her, she seemed as simple as a child, and—now—the Sphinx is twice as easy to understand."

"You remind me of a man I met recently, Victor. He was married about a year ago, and he told me that before he married he feared that the eternal round of daily companionship would make them know each other so well that the monotony of existence would be terrible. But he found that the better he got to know his wife, the stranger she became. Instead of becoming a great commonplace in his life, she became a symbol of the Eternal Mystery. And he added that, if things went on as they were going, they would end by being two complete strangers haunting the same house."

"Well, what do you make of that, Hen?"

"Oh, it's a real marriage, that's all."

"Pretty uncommon things, then, real marriages."

"Very uncommon. The only real thing about many marriages is the divorce."

"Sounds bitter, Hen, for a man with a sense of peace."

"You've worked round to it again, Victor."

"You've got to talk about it."

"All right."

"Now, listen. The trouble is you're not a fool, so you can't be dismissed."

"Dismissing fools, Victor, doesn't explain them."

"I really haven't time to understand fools."

"But, my dear Victor, if you don't understand what a fool is, you may be one yourself without knowing it."

"Oh, all this is part of the sense-of-peace outfit! I know—one suffers fools gladly and all that."

"I only mean, Victor, that it's worth understanding ignorance—your own and other people's."

"I haven't time, dear feller. I'm too concerned with myself, and I'm not afraid of that word 'egotist.' To hell with all that sentimentality about others! You've got to have a basis for your own life before the question of 'others' arises. It's popular to chat about 'others,' and 'one's duty to others,' because all that stuff is so much easier than to have the courage to take the responsibility for one's own life. There are a lot of people going about nowadays telling 'others' what they ought to do, but I've yet to see the man to whom the phrase, 'Physician, heal thyself,' does not apply. It makes me sick—the whole spectacle of life is unreal and degrading."

"Well, what about you? Have you got your basis for life?"

"No; I haven't, and I don't pretend that I have. I'm like a leaf in the wind. I'm at the mercy of every new theory and swayed by every gust of emotion. You say I corner others and try to find out their ideas. I do. They may have what I'm looking for. Anyway, I want to find out what it is in them that makes their lives possible. I simply cannot believe that people are what they appear to be. They can't *live* that! It's impossible. I tell you, Hen, I'm interested only in one thing when I talk to a man or a woman, and that is—what is his or her creed. No, listen! I don't mean when I say 'creed' any rubbish about Church, or what they give out as being their views concerning God. Oh dear, no! I mean the values that really affect their everyday lives."

"You mean, Victor, that you're interested in what people love."

"That's it. That's their creed—what they love. That's often a secret, hidden thing, but it's the sun round which a man's world revolves. I don't care twopence whether it is what is called a vice or a virtue. I want to know what it is. It may be a mistress, it may be drink—the devil alone knows what it may be! And I don't care, but I do want to know what each man lives by, and then I want to see if I could live by it. If people confide in me, Hen, it's because I'm not afraid to tell them about my life. I invite them to play a game of cards with me."

"A game of cards?"

"Yes. In every heart there's a pack of secrets which are hidden from the world. I call them a pack of cards. Well, I deal one of mine, and the odds are a man responds by playing one of his. Then you learn his creed, and it's the real one—not the one he professes. The latter is usually an airy abstraction which no more affects his life than Einstein's theory affects it."

"I see. And now you'd like to get my sense-of-peace under your microscope?"

"Yes—more than anything. I'll tell you why. Every one I know is in a turmoil. Look where you will, everywhere there are signs of amazing discontent and rebellious unrest. Well, the reasons given for this upheaval are clearly totally inadequate. People say that it's caused by poor conditions and so on. Rubbish! Conditions used to be far worse. Then idiots say it's education. Again—rubbish! The poor are still as uneducated as the rich. No, it's deeper than all that. There's a gale raging about the Tree of Life, and every leaf is shaking in the wind. But you, somehow, seem removed from the tempest. You don't seem to be in a turmoil. Well, you're not a fool, so you may have got hold of something. That's what intrigues me —there may be something in this sense of peace of yours."

"Well, I'm easily explained in the terms of your dope theory."

"My—what?"

"Your dope theory, Victor."

"What the devil's that?"

"You always forget your own theories. You held this one strongly a year ago. It was quite an elaborate theory. Give me some more tea."

"Good Lord, man, don't talk about tea! Here, have the pot. What was this dope theory?"

"I'll tell you. I'll make it short, but I must make it complete, and I'm going through with it whether you remember it or not."

"Go ahead."

"You said that each life represents an attempt to escape from the horror of Reality. You asserted that this attempt is common to all lives, and is the only thing which unites them. The method, or means, of escape varies in every possible and conceivable way, but every one makes an attempt to escape."

"Yes, yes, I remember, Hen!"

"Hush! You said, one man tries to escape from the horror of Reality by plunging into debauch. Another takes to drink. Another lives for pleasure. Many people seek the excitement of vice as a means of escape from the Truth. Truth—Reality—you said, was the enemy. Other people seek an escape in making money, being respectable, or doing good works. But there were others, you held, who are more sensitive, and they seek a subtler form of escape. They seek to hide the naked horror of Truth under the magnificent mantles of their own dreams. These are the artists, the philosophers, the dreamers. They dope themselves with the subtle drug of Beauty. But you went farther than this. You said that there was another class still who are too sensitive to be deceived by any of these illusions. You called them the Saints, and you said that no specific drug provides them with an escape from the horror of Truth. You said that, for them, a super-dope is necessary."

"A super-dope. Yes, I remember. Go on, Hen."

"And you said that the saints call their superdope—God."

"Yes. That's right."

"But listen. You didn't stop there; you went on. You said that the few—the saints—who demand the super-dope (which they call God) realize that other men are simply little people for whom a drug of some kind provides a satisfactory means of escape. But the few, whose craving is so great that the super-dope is necessary to satisfy it, went beyond all the other drug-takers in that they claimed that their super-dope is Truth—that they have the Truth—and that the Truth is God. The saints, you said, escape from the horror by saying that it doesn't exist. And I remember you added that, when a man has suffered to the point beyond which it is impossible for him to suffer further, he either commits suicide or else he embraces the last, the greatest, the all-embracing illusion—the illusion of God—the super-dope."

"I say, Hen, you've a good memory."

"Yes—sometimes. Anyway, you summed up your theory by saying that the man who escapes from the bitter reality of life by wasting his substance with harlots and the man who escapes by embracing the idea of God are not essentially different. They are merely deceived by different illusions."

"Yes—well? I think it's about right, Hen. Why repeat it all?"

"Well, you see, I fit into your theory perfectly. I'm one of the super-dope fiends. That explains my sense-of-peace. I have embraced what you call the greatest illusion, and the sense of peace is therefore, according to you, the dream-vision of the super-drug fiend."

"Lord! I've never heard you talk so much before, Hen."

"I've been quoting you—that's why."

"Anyhow, you think my theory is all childish rubbish?"

"It may be the truth, Victor. You may be the only person in the world who is not held by any illusion."

"Oh, shut up, Hen! I'm not even through the illusion of desiring to see the light of a midnight fire dancing over the body of a naked woman. But I know that when I gratify that desire I'm merely running away from the demands of an imperative need within me. That's the point—the drug only half works for me."

"My dear Victor, I think your theory a most ingenious one."

"You can jest at it, if you like, but my theory doesn't make me comfortable. It doesn't allow me to compromise, like all the others, and so find an artificial and fugitive peace. It's not a dope for me, because I don't get even the paradise of a fool out of it. All the dope-takers—no matter what their brand may be—get their little dream of an oasis as they lie sleeping in the desert. You must be fair to the theory."

"I'm fairer to it than you are, Victor. You forgot it. That's unpardonable."

"You can make me look a fool. Nothing's easier—and I don't care. I can easily be made to look very young, very foolish. I know it's easy to laugh at me, and I don't care twopence. I've listened to you repeating that old theory of mine, and it sounds very absurd and conceited and all that—but the root of the whole problem is in it."

"Yes, that's true. It's true in this sense: there's either meaning or madness at the root of things. That's to say, there's either Something to which the best in man is related, or the best in him is just an accident, and no more abiding than the worst things. All is Chance or all is Law. There's no room for anything between the two."

"Right! And if it's Chance, Hen, then life's just an inferno, and my dope theory stands, and men simply spend their lives seeking an artificial dream because they daren't face the meaningless Truth."

"And if all is Law?"

"Oh well, then the theory needs revision. All I mean is that the root of the problem is in it. And until a man knows whether he believes that all is Chance or, alternatively, that all is Law, I say he hasn't a basis for his life. But no one has it out with himself—he's content to have a complete contradiction between his acts and his alleged beliefs. So I ignore his professed beliefs—his real creed is the one he lives. His life shows where he puts his faith. But, Lord, Hen, I'm in a hell of a muddle myself!"

"Go on, Victor."

"I'll show you what I mean. Let's discuss concrete examples; it makes it easier. God! I must smoke. Wait a minute. That's better. All this must bore you to death, Hen."

"It doesn't; go on."

"Well, this is how most people seem to go on in this world: they recognize that there is a law, or principle, underlying certain of their activities, but as regards life as a whole they believe that blind Chance rules their destiny. What I mean is this. Take an engineer. He realizes in his work that he has to conform with the laws governing engineering, and he knows that, if he doesn't, his bridge will fall into the river. Well, if his bridge *does* fall into the river, he doesn't say that it's pure Chance any more than he would claim Chance as a collaborator if the bridge stood. But if our engineer suddenly finds he has cancer, or that his wife dies, or a misfortune of some kind happens to him, he regards it as an accident, and one which might happen to anybody, at any minute."

"You mean, Victor, that he goes on as if his life were divided into two parts, in one of which Law presided, and in the other blind Chance were the ruler."

"Exactly. It never occurs to our engineer that there must be a thousand laws of which we are ignorant for every one about which we know a little; and that, therefore, when an event happens that we do not understand, we should realize that we are confronted by a manifestation of a law. But no! our engineer—like the rest of us—is content to go on living in a world which presents a complete contradiction. In so called practical affairs there is Order: in other departments of life there is Chaos. Well, it seems to me, if cancer is an accident which may descend on any one at any time, for no reason, then the whole of life is an accident, and the laws which govern engineering (and all the other laws men have discovered) are accidents too. I go further—if there is such a thing as an accident at all, everything that happens is an accident. There's Law behind everything or Chance behind everything. What we call an accident is either the working of a law we don't understand—or everything is an accident."

"But, my dear Victor, don't you see that men call those events 'accidents' for which they are not prepared to accept responsibility? Good Lord, man, your engineer is prepared to accept responsibility for his bridge, so he doesn't chatter about Chance. But he won't accept responsibility for his own body. Oh dear, no! He will fling food and drink into it for forty or fifty years without giving a thought as to the wisdom of what he is doing. He will, in fact, treat his body as he would never dream of treating a piece of machinery, and then, when something happens to it—well—then—it's 'old age,' or 'bad luck,' or 'Chance' or something. Besides, you've got to remember that it takes a great faith to believe that *everything* is the result of Law. I don't mean simply to believe it—but to *live* it. That needs a great faith."

"I know that, Hen. But you've got to have a great faith, or none. I see the problem clearly enough. That is, I see this—you can believe that it's all Chance or all Law, but there's no room for anything between the two. Well, I personally believe it's all Chance, despite the Laws men have discovered, because I can't believe that the hell I see around me is the result of Law—I can't believe it, and I don't. I say, therefore, that the Truth is too dreadful for any one to face—hence my dope theory. But these confounded people who compromise with the whole problem, I can't understand them! They seem to regard God as a crippled giant."

"They do, Victor—most of them."

"Oh well, to hell with that! I can't stand that at any price! I'm

not going to dope myself. If the whole thing is hell, then I'm *not* for
making the best of it. Making the best of it!—that's the modern
creed! If the truth about life makes life impossible, then let's put an
end to the whole ghastly farce and stop trying to lend it the beauty
and dignity of tragedy."

"Universal suicide, Victor?"

"Yes. If the truth about life is such that the only thing to do is
to dope yourself into a stupor, well then, let's stop breeding and
die out. Meanwhile, however, these people who regard hideous
disease, war, famine, and pestilence as accidents that may descend
at any moment, are quite prepared to bring children into this hell
of a world. They haven't any faith in life—their own lives are the
living proof of that—but they continue to perform acts which are
only justifiable if they have a mighty faith in life. God above! (if
there is one!) believing what they believe, they are nothing more
than a pack of criminal lunatics, and all the more dangerous
because they appear to be harmless! Bitter? Yes, I am bitter! And
I've no use for those virtues which can only exist if their owner
goes through life in blinkers."

"Never mind about others, Victor; what about yourself?"

"My life is the most ghastly contradiction of all. My mind says
there are no values—none. But my heart still worships at the altars
which my mind has destroyed. That's true, and that's hell. My heart
loves beauty; it loves all earth; and it loves all the high hopes and
mighty cravings of men. It loves on—blindly and without reason.
My mind cries: 'That thing you worship is false; it's a lie!' But my
heart merely repeats its monotonous answer: 'I love, I love, I love.'
Well, one can't go on living like that. But one does go on living like
that. Yes, it's true. My heart urges me to create things of beauty,
and my mind says: 'Ah, so you are like the others. You are going
to make a pretty little garden on the dung-hill. That will be nice.
Another coward has taken *another* allotment in hell.' That's how it
goes on with me—day after day. I'm no better than the rest—I'm
worse. That's why I hate them. A real drunkard always despises the
man who has a fling now and again."

"Well, there's one thing, Victor; you've got a lot off your chest
this afternoon. It will do you no end of good."

"God knows; I don't! So your sense-of-peace comes from this:

you believe that all is Law, and you accept what you don't understand as the working of a law of which you are ignorant."

"Yes."

"And everywhere you see filth, suffering, squalor, and crime?"

"I don't see it everywhere, but I do see it."

"And you accept it, Hen?"

"I'm responsible for it, Victor. I'm guilty too—I share in the general guilt. Look here, we're all in the dock! The whole of humanity is in the dock, and each one of us screams, 'I'm not guilty; the others are guilty!' So we wrangle—fight and accuse each other—while the invisible gods sit in judgment unimpressed by our protestations of individual innocence. We are all guilty."

"You believe that, Hen?"

"I do."

"Do you live it?"

"Evidently not—or you wouldn't have had to ask the question. Come on; we've talked enough."

"Well, look here, Hen. Let's have dinner together. I won't talk about myself any more. We'll talk about nothing. I don't want to be alone."

"All right, Victor, come on. . . ."

I remember how I heard them get up and go slowly downstairs. When they had gone, I rose and looked out of the window. The heaven was a blue dome of dusk, lit by the first faint stars.

§ 8

"Hurrah! there's a blaze! Now on with this log!"

"Oh, Victor, you can't put that tree-trunk on the fire. Are you mad, boy?"

"Yes, Pam! Mad and raving! I'm delirious to-night. On she goes —there! By Heaven, that's something like a fire! Each flame is an inspired tongue praising your beauty. Aha, the blood in my veins has become fire to-night. Don't you move—don't you dare to move! Move! when I've draped the couch with black, and posed your marvellous body upon it so that the light of the leaping flames may caress its wonder and illuminate its mystery! Don't you dare to move. Lie there; be still; don't speak! One moment you look like the goddess of fire and the next you look like a victim on the altar of sacrifice."

"Lord! I do believe I'm with a madman! It's a nice thing to be at the top of this house alone with a madman, at midnight, lying naked on a couch, in a weird room lit only by an enormous fire."

"Hush, woman; don't speak. I'm pondering the eternities."

"I wish you would not call me 'woman.'"

"Child—nymph—spirit—angel—Eve. Take your choice. Don't speak. When you are silent, you are Eternal; when you speak, you are merely a voice in the house of Time."

"Well, don't you speak either!"

"Hush, Pam. That's different—quite different. My voice is the voice of Wisdom. And Wisdom is outside time and space."

"Victor, you are impossible."

"Shut up! How can I spread the magnificence of my imagination before you when you call me impossible? Lie still in the forest of your hair, clad in your robe of flame. Here we dream over the fire. For how many countless centuries has the race of man brooded by night over the fire? How many eyes have gazed into its depths? How many dreams have kindled with the flames and died with them? Cave fires, camp fires, fires of the feast, fires of sacked and burning cities, fires of sacrifice, fires of the hearth—have they not leapt and died in lands over which the waters of the sea now murmur and moan? Have they not blazed at the will of forgotten tribes and perished races? Are they not kindled to-night all over the lands of the living, and do not the ghosts of the dead draw near to them and dream again their dreams? What memory is older in us than that of nights spent by the flames? All the memories of the race stir within us as we look into those blazing logs—memories as old as night and deeper than the years."

"I love you when you don't talk about yourself, Victor."

"I haven't a self to-night. It's gone. I've lost it—it's been driven out. I only hope to God I shan't find it standing by the bed when I wake to-morrow! Your marvellous body inspires me. It's a mirror wherein I glimpse the mysteries, and now and again I see in a flash the shimmer of their eyes behind the shrouding veils. Listen!

> I am not I to-night,
> You are not you:
> Our souls become one light,—
> All things are new."

"Did you make that up on the spur of the moment, Victor?"

"When invention needs a spur, it's all up, Pam. Hush, why will you speak? Your eyes are like the soul of flame. Lord! if we could see all that has been necessary to bring us together here to-night! If we could see that! What cosmic catastrophes, what cataclysms, what destinies! You and I, in this hour—the latest link of an eternal chain. Is this but another tryst between us in an age-long romance, Pam? Have I sought you out countless æons ago? Have I fled from you a thousand times? Have I writhed at your feet when you have bidden me go? Have I laughed at the anguish in your eyes when you sought mercy at my torturing hands?"

"I should think the last is very possible, Victor. I suddenly thought the other night in bed that you're cruel. You've a cruel mouth. In some of your moods I can easily imagine you torturing me. I saw it all quite suddenly when I was in bed the other night."

"I hope you were alone, Pam?"

"I was—thank Heaven!"

"Thank Heaven, you won't be to-night! Do you know, I've an awfully good mind to chuck all your clothes out of the window?"

"Victor, don't be a lunatic."

"It's a good idea—chuck the lot out as a kind of symbolic gesture to the world in general. It would be as if to say: 'Look here, this is what's happening in one house-top, and we don't care a damn who knows it.' It might do good. It might alter the whole life of some dreary fellow who is now prowling about the midnight streets."

"Don't be ridiculous, Victor! Besides, my underclothes have got my name on them."

"Splendid! We'd advertise for their return. We'd put in the papers: '*Lost—Lady's underclothes, bearing the name "Pam." Inadvertently thrown out of the window by a gentleman at midnight in a moment of enthusiasm excusable in the circumstances. Any one returning them will be suitably rewarded by seeing their owner in the state of nature which her loss renders unavoidable.*' There! I'm sure that would make interesting reading. Besides, thousands of liars would arrive with underclothes which they would have marked 'Pam,' and you could accept the lot. We might open a shop."

"I'm really afraid to stay with you, Victor. I am absolutely certain that you have at last gone crazy. This fire is roasting me slowly to death. It's enormous. I wish we'd got some chestnuts."

"Chestnuts! Be quiet! Stop talking! I've a good mind to torture you. Not much—just enough to make you play hide-and-seek with Pain."

"I said you were cruel. You are, too. I know you are. I hate you."

"Here, damn it! we've forgotten that bottle of wine. That's because you talk so much. Where the devil's the corkscrew? Ah, here we are! When I've drunk this, you won't get a chance to speak."

"Give me some first. You've dreadful manners, Victor!"

"Hush, Pam, hush! Look—wine! red wine! See how it glows in the light of the flames like a melted ruby! Come on, let's drink! We can't waste the night in sleep. To-morrow is Sunday—you can go home about mid-day and sleep then, can't you?—that is, of course, provided we don't burn the house down. I drink to you, to Life, and all the old dead gods!"

"You're very jolly to-night, Victor. What's happened to you?"

"Nothing—just nothing. My joy is irrational. Everything is just the same, and yet, for this hour, everything is changed. We won't analyze it. One can only dissect dead things. I take the hour ere it fades. To-night I love with a passion all that I have ever denied. I'd like to clink glasses with God and drink to His universe. I know, of course, that if I went out into those dark streets below us, I should find a world that looks like the efforts of a lunatic and a drunkard working in collaboration; yet I like that world—I love life, I accept it all. My blood has ceased to be a temperate stream: it's become fire. Kiss me to-night, and to-morrow we'll toss to decide whether we go on living or not. Heads—for life; tails—for death."

"Heads for mine, Victor. I'm glad you've thought of kissing me at last. Do you know I've been lying here like this for nearly an hour and you haven't kissed me once yet?"

"Lord, Pam! a kiss is so inadequate. I want to put my arm round the whole world and kiss Life on the lips."

"Kiss me, you lunatic, kiss me!"

"There! there! and there! I believe your body is turning into fire. Ah, lie like that with your eyes closed. You'd look even more beautiful if you were dead, Pam."

"I shall be soon. You're drinking all the wine, Victor. Give me some."

"Here you are. Don't laugh at me, Pam! Why are you laughing?"

"Oh, my dear, you look so strange and wild. Your hair is all over the place, and your eyes flash in the firelight. I believe we've both gone mad. Or perhaps we are dead, Victor. We seem so far away from everything human. And it's so silent here. I believe we're dead."

"I hope so. I drink this to the next world! Yes, to the next world. Hurrah! Do you know, Pam, this world has come to an end, thank God? Yes, it's the end of the world. The world of Time and Space is ended."

"What *do* you mean?"

"It's the greatest joke imaginable. Listen! Every one for centuries had thought that at the end of the world the hills would fall upon them, the mountains would cover them, the earth would be rent, and the stars would fall. And now the end of the world is here—and everything appears to be the same. That's the supreme joke—it appears to be the same."

"What nonsense is this?"

"You're probably right. It's not my own. A man I know called Henderson told me. I've often mentioned him. I call him Hen. Well, he told me. He said it's the end of the world. Whenever a new idea of God is born on earth, the world comes to an end. That's what he said."

"You *do* know some people, I must say! Victor, you child, these people will turn your brain talking all this nonsense to you. I thought this man you called Hen was better than the others."

"He's all right, Pam. He's got a sense-of-peace, although the end of the world has come. That's rather an achievement. It's like walking a tightrope during an earthquake. Hen says that the new idea of God that has been born on earth will transform the world. It's the end of the old values. It's the end of the world!"

"Victor, do you know you are shouting at the top of your voice? For Heaven's sake, be quiet! If people arrive to see what all the noise is about, and find me with no clothes on, and you yelling that it's the end of the world, they may not think that we are entirely normal."

"The tragedy is, my dear, that nine out of ten of them would think they had discovered a scene of desperate vice. Of all the absurdities current in this mad world, the conception as to what constitutes sin is the most absurd. I'll tell you how they got their ideas about sin, Pam. It's not uninteresting. Do you know that there are only two classes of people in the world?"

"Which are they? Victor—and the rest!"

"Be serious, child. I'm educating you. First, I revealed the beauty of your body to you, and now I'm going to develop the potential glories of your mind."

"I see. I shall end a lunatic, too."

"Hush! There are two classes—the vital and the non-vital—the quick and the dead. Well, the non-vital were terribly afraid of the vitality of the others, so they termed all expressions of that vitality as 'sins.' Thus, if a man loved a woman, and they became lovers and didn't marry, they were 'sinners.' If a man or woman claimed that he or she heard the voice of God direct, and not through the medium of some tongue-tied priest, that one was a heretic—a 'sinner.' If a man, because of the life leaping in his veins, rose to deny the current institutions which fettered life, he was a revolutionary—a 'sinner.' And so on. All the great gestures of the human spirit were 'sins.' Life was a 'sin'; death was virtue. The little people made it all so simple. Well, that nonsense is over. The little people are the sinners—the only ones. The very things they claim as virtues are the only sins. The little mean thoughts, the little fearful lives, the daily denials of everything that rises above the dead level of monotonous existence, the whole mean little philosophy of 'safety'—those are the sins. And the heaven of which the little dead people dream—that is hell. And the god they worship in their hideous chapels and churches—he is the devil. I tell you, Pam, the whole horrible little tribe has been found out, and their day is over. And they know it. Deep in their dead hearts they know it, and—my God! what a frenzy of fear they are in! They ramp and rage about demanding the 'strong hand'; the suppression of 'dangerous' doctrine, the abolition of thought, the

revival of every form of the old tyranny. But the word has gone
forth against them and they know it. The day of the hypocrites is
over. Always they have denied growth, and now they who have
cumbered the ground too long have got to give place. They have
made the world a sepulchre, but Life is rising from the dead."

"What a funny boy you are, Victor! You're enthusiastic to-night.
You believe in things. You're not bitter—even when you judge
others you're not bitter—and yet, as a rule, you're black, destruc-
tive, and horrible. Two men live in your body."

"They are foes, Pam. They fight together. Day in, day out, they
fight, each one striving for mastery. It is a fight to the death—and
each one knows it."

"You're a dramatic person, Victor."

"Life's dramatic, Pam—damned dramatic. Yes, they fight, these
two. And then suddenly, to-night, they disappear, and I am one—
whole. Thoughts and emotions flow through me; they are born
and they find immediate expression. I feel impersonal. That's what
I meant when I said I had no 'self' to-night."

"Do you know, Victor, I often think you're intoxicated by words?
Yes, I do. Words—ideas—they are everything to you. I can't express
it, but they are 'things' to you—more real than anything else."

"Let's have an example, Pam."

"Well, wait a minute. Let's think. I haven't your gift of the gab,
my dear. You go on like a gramophone with a dictionary for a
record."

"I don't want any insults, Pam. I want an example. The hours
pause to gaze at your white beauty, and pass onward to Eternity,
turning to look back on one of Time's miracles."

"There we are! That's an example! Shut up! Don't talk, or I shall
forget what I'm going to say. Now you don't care twopence about
my body really."

"Well, I am damned! You infidel! Come, the fire is kindled. I
must burn you at the stake."

"No, it's true, Victor. You get me here like this for two reasons.
One is, it gives you a kind of pride to see me like this; and the
other is, that you can praise my body with words. But you find
greater beauty in your words than in their subject. You child! You
talk about desire and passion for me. Rubbish! I know what most

men are, and what they want. You're not like that. You only do all
that because you think you might be missing something. You're
quite conventional, in a way. So many men are mad on sleeping
with women that you think there must be something in it. But,
really, you don't care a bit about any of that."

"I say! And you said you hadn't the gift of the gab!"

"Shut up, Victor!"

"My dear, in the highest circles people don't shout 'Shut up!' at
each other."

"There's no need to, Victor. In the highest circles people haven't
anything to say."

"By Jove, that's very bright of you, Pam. You're rather witty,
you know."

"You're a condescending little beast. But what I say is true. You
only want to talk, Victor. You only ever write anything because
you can't always find a listener."

"I've never been so insulted in my life."

"It's true, every word of it. I'm beginning to know you, Victor.
You talk on and on. You find words about the beauty of my body
till I feel as if I were clothed in a garment of speech. You go on,
hour after hour, and then you kind of pinch yourself and think,
'There she is—naked. Of course now one takes her to bed. That's
the thing to do. If I simply talk and leave it at that, I'd be a fool,
because every one would say I was a fool.' That's how you look at
it, really."

"I don't think I like you very much, Pam. I used to think you
were a simple, natural girl, with a nice affectionate nature. But
I'm not so sure about it. You seem to have no respect for the usual
decencies and reticencies of civilization."

"Oh, of course there are other things, too. One side of your
imagination is diseased and suggests all kinds of impossible sensations to you. And you try to test some of them in life—with me,
in fact."

"You know, Pam, this conversation is really not decent. One
couldn't put it in a book, for instance."

"Oh, one could nowadays, Victor. You know that—don't be
absurd! People have had to become human again—the perfection
fake became impossible."

"You know you really are coming out a bit, Pam."

"My dear, do you think all this talk with you hasn't wakened me up? I love you and I hate you. I suppose I love one of the men in you, and hate the other."

"You're a darling, Pam."

"But you remember what I say about not caring for anything but the joy you experience in expressing your thoughts and feelings in words. It's true."

"I expect you're right. What a curious girl you are, Pam! But isn't what you say about me true about every one, in its degree? I don't mean they love words and ideas, because the Lord knows they don't. But all of us, in our different ways, try to express the emotions that life wakes within us. We all try to give our answer to life, so to speak. Most of us aren't conscious of this—but what the devil does that matter? The point is—we all do it. We are confronted by the totally amazing spectacle of life. We gaze in utter bewilderment at it, and then something is born in us and whispers: 'In all life's chaos, I desire this. This is what I value; it is my god.' We may not even hear the whisper, but it's there and it moves us. And then we seek to give a form to what we love. Oh, of course, the forms are infinite. It may be the birth of a child, it may be the birth of a book. It may be the striking of a blow at a wrong, it may even be a suffering for which no word or no tear is found. It may be anything. A murder, madness—anything. But we create an image of what we are, and as we grow and develop the image alters. So that to-day we deny what yesterday we affirmed. But we all make an answer to life, and that answer springs from what we love. There are as many worlds as there are men and women. No two mirrors reflect identically the same thing."

"I love you to-night, Victor."

"God has thrown this hour to us, as we toss a coin to a beggar. We are living it together, Pam."

"So you agree with what I said about you?"

"Yes, it's true. But you're not to make capital out of the fact that I agree with you. I still need you, Pam, you—the warm, white reality. The words are not enough by themselves—yet."

"I always give you your own way, Victor. That would be all right if you always knew what you wanted. But you deceive yourself as to what you want. I say, are we ever going to bed?"

"No—never. I'm going to put another log on the fire, and there's still wine left."

"All right. Go on. I don't care. I'm happy to-night. Do you know, my dance went awfully well at the show to-night."

"Do your dance for me here, Pam."

"Now, my dear boy? Strange as it may seem to you, I do wear some clothes on the stage. Not many, it's true, but still—some."

"Yes, that's all right; but the dance—the essential dance—takes place underneath them. Dance your dance as you are now. I never wanted what the public wants."

"All right. Move that chair. But I haven't the music, Victor."

"Well, hum the tune. Go on. Ah, that's right. You can dance, Pam. I know nothing whatever about dancing, but you can dance. Ah, that's beautiful. Yes, you are dancing as one should dance—you feel that you have made contact with the rhythm of life. It's a great medium. It's older than speech, deeper than thought. Go on—don't listen to me. Yes, dancing is a great medium. When the first heart thrilled with the joy of life, the limbs leapt in eager and rhythmic response. I'm certain that dancing was the first language, and it conveys all that cannot be expressed through the tyranny of set speech. There! Splendid, Pam! By the Lord God, if managers had eyes—which they haven't—you'd be a real star amid the constellations of the over-advertised obscure."

"Lord, boy, let me sit down! I don't usually give two shows a night. Well, that's my dance, Victor; do you like it?"

"Like it! don't be absurd! You look like the spirit of Life leaping through a cemetery. It's curious, isn't it, how people pay to see an expression of what they have killed in themselves?"

"I wish I got a bigger share of what they do pay, Victor."

"So do I. But it always fascinates me to see an audience. They seem to be paying others to live for them. They kill things in themselves in order to get money, and then they spend the money to watch an expression of those very things they have destroyed in themselves. Then they applaud, go home, and count their money. I am the only person in the whole wide world who understands the strange poverty of the rich."

"Now, Victor, you're getting conceited again."

"Sheer, sober fact, Pam. The poverty of the rich!"

"What are you talking about? What do you call poverty?"

"Any one is poor, Pam, who is always thinking about money. Hence the poverty of the rich. Do you know, it's heart-rending to stay in the big houses of the capitalists?"

"But you can't be speaking from experience, my dear boy."

"Unfortunately—yes. I have passed days and nights in the mansions of the rich. They are mental slums. The greatest pauper is the beggar in purple. I cannot tell you what I suffered."

"But I never knew that you had any rich friends, Victor?"

"I had, my dear, but they had to drop me. They simply couldn't afford to keep up with me. I led them into such extravagance."

"Oh, do talk sense, Victor!"

"Absolute truth. My vitality made such demands on their vitality that they couldn't afford it. Really, they couldn't. Their account was overdrawn at the Bank of God. Trying to live up to me, they drew cheques which were not met. They had to economize. They couldn't afford me. They dropped me. And then, once again, all their little remaining store of vitality was employed in digesting the enormous meals they consumed—four times a day, at fixed and unalterable intervals. I know something about the poverty of the rich, my dear! And even now, in charitable moments, I often throw them the odd coppers of my vitality so that they can go and buy themselves a dream."

"Madman!"

"Darling!"

"Victor, don't shout like that. You'll wake the dead."

"Rubbish, Pam; they are all in bed and asleep."

"That's where we ought to be."

"Oh no, Pam! There are flowers that only open at night—rare flowers that only show their beauty to the stars. They are the secret thoughts of the old, dreaming earth. And in our minds, too, there are thoughts that only blossom beneath the beams of the moon. By day we believe in, and serve, the madness of men; but when night comes we bring secret offerings and spread them silently on the ruined altars of the forgotten gods. Don't talk about sleep, Pam; it is blasphemy. Besides, there's some wine left."

"Well, let's drink it, Victor. For Heaven's sake, don't put any more on that fire! How you can stand the heat with all those clothes on, I cannot imagine. You'll set this whole rickety house on fire before you've done."

"Here's your share of the wine, and don't insult the fiery furnace. And don't bother in the least if the house catches fire. It's not of the slightest importance. You ought to be used to it by this time."

"You really are off your head, Victor!"

"Of course you ought to be used to living in a burning house. We all ought to be used to it. What are these bodies of ours but houses on fire? Besides, the great house of Civilization is ablaze. It denied the lightning and it has been struck by the lightning. It's ablaze, I tell you! Meanwhile all its occupants sit eating and drinking, plotting and planning, and say to each other: 'There's no such thing as fire—it's a vulgar superstition.' And all the time the house is ablaze, and unless its inhabitants wake up, the damned roof will fall on their thick heads. Hooray!"

"I believe you're drunk, Victor."

"What! on half a bottle?"

"You've had more than half. I've tried to mention that fact several times, but couldn't get a word in. Drunk's the wrong word—you're intoxicated. It's partly the wine, partly the heat, and chiefly—words! You're intoxicated with yourself, boy."

"Rubbish! I'm intoxicated with you, Pam. There you stand by the fiery furnace, looking like the white flame of the spirit that is born of the red flames of the fire. I drink to you, Pam, I drink to you!"

"Listen! We must go to sleep, do you know that? Yes, really. I'm going to jump into bed, and so are you. And we are going to sleep—do you understand?"

"I am listening. I won't say more than that."

"I am going to go to sleep—with my head on your shoulder. Let's do that to-night, Victor."

"Well—without prejudice?"

"Don't know what that means."

"It isn't to constitute a precedent?"

"Don't know what *that* means."

"You're the devil, Pam! I give it up. You shall have your own way."

"I love you, Victor!"

"I love you, Pam! I say!"

"What?"

"We might talk a bit more in bed. We'll smoke a bit and just chat. What do you think?"

"All right."

"I say! It didn't take you long to get in, Pam."

"Well, I had only one garment—to put on."

"Yes, that's true. I shan't be a minute. I think the fire will do as it is. Here, take the cigarettes and the matches. We shall want them. It's a pity the wine's finished. But there it is—nothing lasts. Now I wonder where the devil those pyjamas are. I bought a new pair in your honour. Ah, here they are!"

"It's just like you to get scarlet pyjamas, Victor."

"I expect I shall look extraordinarily attractive in them."

"Rubbish! You talk too much for any one to remember that you have a body."

"I wish I could forget it so easily, Pam. I regret to say that it has a remarkable number of different ways of reminding me of its existence. In fact, frequently it succeeds in making me believe that it's the only reality. I say, it's quite warm by this fire with very little on!"

"I have been telling you so for hours. You never believe anything, Victor, till you experience it yourself."

"Well, a thing isn't true for you until you do experience it yourself. Now for those pyjamas! There! What do you think of that?"

"You look like the devil, Victor. Particularly with those flames from the fire leaping all around you."

"Good! Make room for the devil, and give him a cigarette. Smoke is his element."

"I'll smoke one—only one—and then we must go to sleep."

"It's awful to think that another day is on its way to us! Dawn and Night—the two extremes between which the pendulum of God's clock swings. By Jove, aren't you warm, Pam!"

"Not uncommon, my dear, when one has been roasted over an open furnace. Your face does look funny! It keeps appearing and vanishing according to the mood of the fire."

"Oh Lord, Pam! soon it will be to-morrow, and all the glory of that fire will be a heap of dull ashes, and the dawn will look in at the window, and it will all be over."

"Be quiet! Why do you want something that will last? You always rave because everything ends."

"Pam, child, I can't really believe in anything that ends. That's my tragedy. Persistence is proof of reality. Only illusions come to an end. But to the devil with all that! Your face looks awfully funny, too. Kiss me. You're very obedient to-night. The difference between men and women is——"

"I say, Victor, not again!"

"Shut up, confound it, or I shall forget! The difference between men and women is that if a woman wants, say, a hundred pounds, she goes and gets it, and then she doesn't mind wasting a few odd shillings. But a man thinks he'll get the hundred pounds by scraping the odd shillings together."

"I don't know what on earth you're talking about, Victor."

"I don't know that I do, but I mean that you are obedient—or generous—because you've got your own way to-night. Of course, you've managed to make me believe that in getting your own way I've really had mine. You know, of course, that men are the most helpless creatures when dealing with women?"

"I hadn't noticed it, Victor."

"My dear, men are children! Children!—all of them. What are called evil men are really simply wicked children. Some play with their toys all their lives and others break them—that's the only difference between men. But—women! My God! damned few of them are children."

"How d'you mean?"

"Well, men run all over the place chasing theories of every kind—women don't. There's the devil of a conspiracy between women—all the more efficient because it's unconscious. They are collectively the most powerful trade union in the whole world. They are such a mighty trade union that they never have to go on strike to get what they want."

"Do you know that when you talk it really is like listening-in to a lunatic asylum?"

"I haven't promised not to smack you—so you'd better be careful. Yes, Pam, women are the devil! The first great triumph of their trade union was when they managed to convince men that men were the stronger sex. The moment men believed that lie, they were done for. They became so conceited that they fell into every trap that a woman set for them; and when a woman helped a man out of the trap she had set for him, she convinced him that *he* was rescuing *her*. Marvellous! A woman always gets her own way by convincing her man that it's what he wants. And the poor idiot believes her! I see it going on all around me. Women are as strong as water."

"Pull yourself together, Victor! You mean—as weak as water."

"No; I do not! I mean as *strong* as water. I believe an old Chinaman once revealed the obvious truth that nothing is as strong as water. It's strong for two reasons: nothing can resist its ceaseless energy and, as it always takes the lowest place, everything—eventually—falls into it. Women are like water and as powerful."

"Do you talk to yourself when you are lying here alone in bed at night, Victor?"

"No; I used to, but one night I said something so funny that I laughed out loud. And the sound of my own laugh frightened me. It was absolutely terrifying. If you don't believe me—you try it. A sudden, spontaneous laugh in the middle of the night when you're alone. You feel afterwards as if Death were sitting on the edge of the bed feeling your pulse."

"Ugh! Aren't you horrible? Well, any more remarks about women?"

"Certainly, Pam. The least one can do when a lady has been gracious enough to reveal to one her naked beauty is to respond by revealing the naked truth in regard to her entrancing sex. By the way, that's the first time you've ever asked me to go on talking."

"Yes. I think I might drop off if you go on. Your voice is very soothing. Victor!—you've no right to pinch me like that! It will leave a bruise."

"Well, Pam, it's surely one that will only be seen in exceptional circumstances."

"Idiot!"

"Angel!"

"Well, I'll finish my remarks about women—then you can go to sleep. Where was I? Oh yes. A woman will forgive anything in a man except his understanding of the method by which she gets her own way. That's why women and the artist type of men have such terrible rows. They are a damned sight too like each other. Now, my view is—— By Heaven, Pam! you've gone to sleep! Well—I'm damned! See how certain the creature is of her power!"

"Victor, dear, I'm certain you're awfully tired—you must want to go to sleep. I'm really only considering you when I doze off."

"From the power and subtle lies of women, Good Lord, deliver me!"

§ 9

I know it is weakness to harp on the impossibility of the task I have undertaken. After all, only two courses are open to me. One is to collect all the notes I have ever made of the conversations I have overheard, and to publish them without explanation or comment; and the other is to make a selection from these notes, and to present them in the form of a confession. (Strange as it may seem, this book is a confession.) Having decided that to select was the only possible course, I should abide by my decision and cease to lament its difficulties.

But I, who spend my days reading and re-reading the large manuscript in my room, frequently discovering additional sheets in quite unsuspected places, am like a man surrounded by memories from which there is no escape. For the majority of us, thoughts, happenings, dreams fall from us, to linger awhile in the sieve of Memory, and then gradually slip through into nothingness. So that most of us, at any particular moment of our lives, are concerned only with the destination at which we have arrived; the roads we have travelled on the journey thither are forgotten. My case is different. I know, only too well, what has happened to my life and where I stand to-day, but I also have a written record of each stage of my journey. In my case, therefore, Memory was not a sieve; it was a manuscript. And the more I read these sheets, the more I realize how subtly and inevitably my own life slipped from me, and how I became merely a spectator of the life of this man Victor, who had dropped from the blue into the room next to mine.

Remember this when you read this book, and try to imagine what your position would be if you possessed a written statement—or a *conscious* memory—of each stage of your own development, so that you could trace the whole process of your growth from what you were to what you are.

I am certain that it was the youth of this man Victor that first fascinated me. He was so young, not in the usual sense of the word, but in a sense that seemed to be strange and of great significance to me. How can one explain? I felt that his youth meant the death of mine, and that is why I hated him. And yet, before long I am certain that an element of pity entered into my hatred. He was young in a special sense—so young that I felt that life held no possible place for him, and that, however confident and bold his speech might be, he was alone—utterly and completely alone. And I felt this, too: that, notwithstanding his jests and the sudden flame of merriment that leapt from him, he was—underneath—at desperate grips with Powers who were seeking to destroy him utterly. And in that conflict he was alone—fighting he knew not what.

I know now that this feeling in me was not awakened by the fact that he questioned everything and was in revolt against life. Gradually, indeed, what he actually said became only of interest to me in so far as it served to indicate the fluctuations of this inner conflict which was occurring in the very depths of his nature. I felt that my destiny was being fashioned in the fire of that conflict. I hated him and I pitied him. I pause in my writing to gaze with morbid interest at the wall which separates us, and I am amazed to remember that, for years now, it has been the only material barrier between us—and yet we have never looked each other in the eyes. And I know now that we shall never meet, that for some utterly inscrutable reason I am destined never to see the man who is responsible for the revolution in my life. So certain am I of this, that for some time now I have ceased those elaborate precautions which I used to employ to avoid the possibility of an accidental meeting. So that—although it is true that I go out but seldom—I go and return at will, with an absolute faith in my conviction that we shall never meet.

Nothing is more terrible in life than to feel that one is divorced from one's own will and that, therefore, the possibility of action is removed, and one passes one's days and nights in a great void, where one waits until the forces before which one is power less indicate the way down which one is to move like an automaton. To stand apart from one's own life, to watch it in a detached and disinterested manner—like a bored spectator at a play—is neither to live nor to die, but it is to haunt the no-man's-land which lies between Life and Death. I have lived like that. In the space of a few brief years I have passed from the belief that every experience was a possibility for me to the conviction that I am totally divorced from all modes of experience, and that the very shape of my own existence is determined by the life of another man.

Although I felt convinced that an inner conflict was proceeding in this man Victor, and although I felt that the issue of this conflict was of supreme importance to his life and to mine, yet I should have found it impossible to state the issues around which this conflict raged. But because I was aware that it existed, I found it easy to reconcile the fierce and bitter moods of his despair with those moods of childish and spontaneous gaiety that to others appeared to be so irreconcilable. I felt, too, that although certain of the explanations he gave of his own conduct seemed sometimes to reveal that he, too, was conscious of the warfare within him, yet I felt that in reality he had no conception whatever of what was happening to him, or of the actual danger which menaced him on all sides. It was my realization that this was so that first woke pity in me for him, and then I began to see how ignorant he was of the standards of the world in which he was living, and how impossible he found it to repose any trust in the things of this earth.

It was not long before I ceased to be deceived by his apparent gaiety, for I soon detected an element in it that did not belong to joy, and I understood that much of his jesting was really but a defiant gesture made in the direction of an invisible foe. I felt that he was pretending to himself that he had gained a freedom which he knew he had not earned. It was a respite from himself.

But much that I say concerning what I detected lurking beneath what he said must necessarily remain obscure to an outsider, because there were many conversations recorded by me which it is not possible to publish. It is necessary that this should be understood.

This man Victor, who has lived next door to me for all these years in complete ignorance of my existence, has, in fact, dictated his autobiography to me. I know more of him than he knows himself, and infinitely more than any of his friends. I soon discovered that to each of his friends he revealed only one side of himself. (Whether he was aware of this I don't know, and it matters little.) But what saved him from any charge of insincerity was the fact that the side of himself which he revealed to the person, with whom he happened to be, was a true presentation of that aspect of his personality. It was not the whole man, but it was not a mask. Never have I known any one influenced in so curious a way by his friends as this man Victor, and I remember that at one time I was convinced that he was most himself with the girl Pam, although I was equally certain that he was totally unaware of the fact. In his holiday moods, the whole man was revealed—in fancy dress. And although I have never seen a line of anything he has written, I know that his writing does not reveal him. Into it, I am certain, he has put only a department of himself.

Yes, he has dictated his autobiography to me. How utterly fantastic that is! He has done, without knowing it, what countless writers have failed to do. He has dictated his confessions. How many have tried to write their confessions, yet all have failed! It is an impossible task. There are a thousand reasons why this is so. Men will set down the truth, but the background is false. Or they will omit to state an essential because they are ashamed, or because there are thoughts of which they are afraid. And, above all, who in retrospect can recapture the precise atmosphere which lent colour and emotion to the thoughts and illusions of the dead years? Men either forget entirely the problems which persecuted them in the past, or they remember them with a smile. With an effort, they may force themselves to realize that once these problems were real to them, but if they attempt to create these problems in writing, their present unreality is immediately apparent. The only possible method is the one adopted, all unconsciously, by this man Victor. To be overheard by one unknown and unseen, who sets down all the intimate conversations uttered over a period of years, is the best method of furnishing a record of each stage of one's development, and of preserving something of the original atmosphere surrounding the successive stages of one's growth. And though even by this method the whole man is not revealed (since, in all of us, our secret is hidden in our silence), yet the reality of each phase of his development is preserved, and, above all, the spontaneity of its original expression is not lacking. What happens to us—the bare fact—is nothing. Our response to it, what it awakes in us, is all.

And so I, sitting here, am surrounded by a record of this man Victor, such as he himself does not possess. I smile when I remember how indignantly he would deny much of what is recorded here—how he would dismiss as a pose a conviction that he once cherished as the soul of Truth. We are all the same—we acclaim the flower and deny the seed. To-day we are ashamed of yesterday, and to-morrow we shall deny to-day.

Here, then, is the greatest difficulty which I have to face: I cannot present the most significant of the data at my disposal. To some of those with whom he has spoken, this man Victor has expressed thoughts which we others—if we have them—never clothe in words. He has stripped thoughts and emotions of which we others are either ignorant or ashamed. He has dared to confront and destroy—I wonder if he will ever find the strength to create. He himself is unaware of all that which he has rejected, for he has rejected nearly all those things by which men live. He has gone naked into a wilderness. Will he find a Truth to clothe him, and the will to create his temple? I do not know, but I do realize that it is not I alone who am responsible for the inadequacy of my representation of Victor.

It has been forced in upon me more and more of late that many of the notes I have of Victor's life, which best reveal certain aspects of it, must be passed over; but it will be necessary in the writing of this narrative to insert, here and there, a page—or speech—torn from its context, in the hope that, even in this mutilated form, it may prove illuminating. Somehow I have to paint as full a portrait of the man as possible and, for the rest, I must suggest at intervals the effect that his life had upon me. And in the attempt to do this, it may well be that you will find nothing of import in the life of Victor, and only a mild amazement will be born in you that his life can have had any effect upon mine. The experience that you and I share in common will decide.

§ 10

The following is an excerpt from a conversation between Victor and another man called Howard. I have no idea as to how long ago this conversation took place, nor do I regard it as being of the smallest importance, but I do remember that, so far as my knowledge goes, the man Howard has not been again to see Victor. One other detail is clear in my memory. I know that the night upon which this conversation occurred there was a dense fog, and that only muffled and far-off sounds rose from the double darkness of the streets below. . . .

"It's impossible for you to go, Howard. You'll have to sleep here. It's black as pitch. The devil is putting up in this town for the night."

"All right. The devil's no bad judge—he knows where he'll get a welcome. God! a night like this wakes things in me!"

"What sort of things?"

"Desires, my boy, beyond the reach of satisfaction. I don't think I'll tell you, Victor. If you were in one of your moods when you look like hell, I wouldn't mind. But to-night you look rather saintly, and that doesn't inspire me much."

"Oh, rubbish, Howard! Don't talk rot. I'm as murky as you, I dare say. Pass the drinks and let's say what we've got to. Either that, or sleep—there's nothing between one or the other."

"Oh, bother sleep! Here's your drink. I'm going to write a book one day, Victor. And unlike most authors, I'm only going to write one."

"I'd like to read it. What's the theme?"

"Well, first of all, the central figure will be a saint."

"Good God! That'll make considerable demands on your imagination, won't it?"

"You wait a bit, Victor. This cove of mine will live like a saint, and people will regard him as one, but in reality he is a sinner beyond all ordinary conceptions of sin. He's the type whose sin (if there were such a thing) is enacted wholly in his imagination, simply because the realities of life are far too limited for him to express his desires in their terms. Do you see what I mean?"

"I think so. Go on."

"Yes, but you must get this clear, Victor. A man who had a pretty big influence on me when I was young really gave me the germ of the idea. He said this: 'An *imaginative* man cannot sin. Only dull people are catered for in sin—as in everything else. This is a *table d'hôte* world.' Well, I thought over that—God knows why!—and I've come to the conclusion that he was right. D'you get what I'm driving at?"

"It's not altogether news to me, Howard. I've often thought you were a bit like it yourself. I am, too. Perhaps it's what we have in common. You mean this—don't you?—that lust can't exist in a human relationship because, by its very nature, it's inhuman. Pornographic literature exists to supply the demands of the imaginative sinner."

"Ah, so you've thought that out, Victor, have you? Yes, that's right. Well—damn what I was saying about the book for a minute! I'll give you an example. Do you know what I'd like to do *now*—if I were here alone?"

"No—what?"

"This. I'd like to go down into the darkness of those streets. There I'd like to see—if the cursed fog would let me!—a woman of quite damnable beauty. I won't describe it, because it always bores the other man cold, simply because he has his own conception as to what constitutes the damnable."

"Well, let's accept that she's the perfection of your damnable type. Go on, Howard."

"Well, I'd simply look at her. Not speak—that's most important—and she wouldn't speak either. But she'd just walk back with me here in silence through the darkness. We'd come up the stairs, and come into this room. And then—well—then—she'd just be my Thing. Do you understand?—my *Thing*. Simply the necessary instrument for the expression of my imaginings. Nothing more—nothing whatever. And then—afterwards—she'd go. I'd stand here and listen to her going downstairs. I'd hear the door bang and the sound of her footsteps die away. And never, never would I see her again. And not one word would have passed between us. There! you're the first man I've ever told that to. Do you understand? It's true—absolutely and literally true. I was always like it. What's called 'the real thing'—well, it's *table d'hôte*, as my friend said. Now can you weave that outlook into a philosophy, Victor?"

"Rather! A philosophy of lust ought to be written. Oh yes, that's simple enough."

"Well, go on. The fact that you understand me has certain implications, Victor."

"I acknowledge them all. They can put the truth about me upon the hoardings for all I care. I am that I am, and I can't be excluded from life—because I'm a part of it. They can sweep me away if they like, but they're only brushing the dirt into a place where it won't show."

"That's all they care about, Victor. A narrow frontage and a private view of heaven—that's the ideal of the frightened little swine. Damn them! Give me a philosophy to embrace what I told you."

"Oh well, your damnable, silent woman—who appears from the night and vanishes into it—she's only an image of your lust, and its refusal to accept any human responsibility. Your damnable woman is most easily explained by considering her opposite—a real, living woman who gives herself to you. What happens in that case is this. You may start simply by desiring her, but it soon ceases to be simple. She *does* speak—possibly quite a lot! She's a name of her own, too, and you can't help knowing that name. At that moment she's no longer your image. She's herself. She's already getting human, you see. And the more you get to know her, the more you are forced—absolutely forced—to realize that she's just such a human being as you are."

"Yes, that's the devil of it, Victor. It's all useless."

"You find out that she's not simply an instrument upon which your imagination can play several variations on certain well-known themes. Either you've got to chuck her, and very quick—in which case you return to your unaided imagination—or you've got to realize her humanity. And, well, when you do that, the other thing is impossible—absolutely impossible. Lord, man, have you never studied the progress of normal men from lovers to fathers? It's the same thing on another level."

"My dear Victor, I've never studied the normal, and I never shall. It may be jealousy—but I loathe them. They make it so easy for themselves, labelling all their desires and vices as 'natural.' Damned pack of lunatics, all suffering from the same type of insanity, as you once said! Ugh! But you're right in what you say. Dead right! It's a hell of a problem."

"Of course, Howard, you realize that your damnable lady, if she lurked conveniently in the fog, wouldn't do, either? You'd soon imagine something more remote and utterly impossible. Lust is a ladder every rung of which breaks under your foot."

"Well, Victor, you certainly understand the state I've explained. What's your remedy?"

"You don't see an escape simply because you understand how the rope got round your neck."

"Yes, that's all right, Victor. But if you understand at all, it's because you've got it in you. Well, how do you get on? You manage somehow."

"Pooh! In this world we do the impossible. People say, 'You must do what you can.' Rubbish! You must do what you can't. Half of us say it's impossible for us to 'live like this,' but we go on. We do the impossible. And the other half enter into a huge conspiracy never to have any time to think about anything. They solve the problem by perpetual movement—like the squirrel in his revolving cage. But if I understand nothing else, Howard, I do understand all the underworld of secret desire and sex aberration."

"All of it! You must have quite an interesting life."

"Oh yes; it's interesting enough. But it amuses me when I'm told that this is a tolerant age in regard to sex. People are a good deal too interested in it to be tolerant. Besides, drowning men are not tolerant towards each other."

"What the devil do you mean by that, Victor?"

"It doesn't matter. But one thing is certain: if you seek to exploit sex as a means of procuring sensation, the only limit to your activities is that created by your own fear."

"I don't know what the devil you're talking about."

"Yes, you do, Howard. No one better. This is how it works. You start by finding the *table d'hôte* of the normal tame. Your imagination suggests all sorts of refinements—many of which are not ordinarily obtainable even *à la carte*. Well, you procure one. You get your new sensation. Then obviously, after a while, repetition dulls its flavour. It becomes commonplace—normal—for you.

Right! You try something else. You go on from one refinement (I love the way people use that word for these things!) to another. If you stand aghast before certain enormities, that's only because you lack the courage to go to the end of your road. Once you admit sensation as an end, why shouldn't you employ any and every means to procure it?"

"Oh well, Victor, I suppose you must draw the line somewhere."

"Why? If you do draw the line somewhere, you're like a counterfeiter who'll make half-crowns, but draws the line at making one-pound notes. The same principle is involved. Anyway, if you set out to search for sensation, you've either got to go on or go back. If you remain stationary, your aberration becomes your norm—to you."

"That's very helpful! Where do you go—if you go back?"

"My dear Howard, to go back is to renounce your original principle. That is, you realize that the search for new sensations begins in illusion, leads towards an infinite series of illusions, and culminates in a state in which any sensation is an impossibility."

"Well, you've certainly thought a bit about mental sensuality. What I'd like to know about you, Victor, is this: are you a saint in the making, or a really first-class sinner ready made?"

"I'll let you know when I find out, Howard. We've all made both words pretty meaningless—but then we've made everything pretty meaningless."

"Anyway, I don't see much in that idea of yours about going back. One can't just tear things out of oneself because one's mind sees, in moments, that they are illusions."

"Course you can't, Howard. The thing is part of a bigger problem. You can't settle it on its own. We all try to. We divide our lives into compartments, isolate our problems, and then try to solve each separately. It's hopeless. There's either something that makes the whole thing organic or there's nothing—in which case we're wasting our time. It's no damned use to tear a branch from the Tree of Life, break it into pieces while it is withering in our hands, and then ponder as to how to make it bear fruit. If your life as a whole has a principle—which is not obtained by the arbitrary creation of a mental scheme to justify the universe—then you'll get a perspective throughout your life. And not otherwise."

"Um! You got that principle yet?"

"No. I shouldn't be sitting here talking if I had. I'd have something to do. But never mind all that! How were you going to end your book, Howard?"

"Oh yes—the book! Well, as I told you, my main character would live like a saint outwardly, while inwardly his imaginings would be suitable themes for frescoes in hell. But the other characters in the book, like people in life, judge him by his exterior. They look up to him. They admire his strength. And he's strong, in his way. They confide in him. He obtains power over them. They come and confess their sins to him. They provide for all his material wants. The women particularly reverence him. He has such a strangely beautiful and spiritual face. Moreover, his voice is very attractive, and he says such wonderful things to them. He's a glory moving amid the squalor of their mean, humdrum little lives. They regard him as a kind of bridge leading to heaven. And he towers above them all, looking down at them with inscrutable, merciless eyes; and he lifts his beautiful, white, womanish hands, with their jewelled fingers, above them all, and he blesses them."

"That's very dramatic, Howard. What next? How do you end it?"

"They find him out. In their midst is a girl of great beauty—a radiant creature, with eyes like stars—who is deceived by him. That's not surprising; all the others also are deceived. She comes to him, and he becomes her spiritual adviser. Any doubts that arise in her heart—and they do arise—she crushes. No one, she feels, could look so beautiful without being beautiful. And he, gazing on her, thinks that perhaps with her he could find food dainty enough for the dreams of his imagination. He sets out to captivate and subdue the whole province of her mind. He hypnotizes her so subtly that she becomes flexible to the least quiver of his will. Before long his voice becomes to her as the voice of God. She ceases to question anything. She yields the depths of her nature to him. And then, with a subtlety of which the world knows nothing, he removes from her heart the ideal of heaven which it cherishes, and insinuates in its place the ideal of his own hell. First, he establishes his sovereignty in her soul, her mind, and her heart, and then, when she is wholly his, he debauches her body with every perversion of his own utterly perverse and pitiless nature."

"I say! that's very pretty. How do the others find out?"

"She goes into the market-place, where his glorious house stands, and as he comes down the steps in all his pomp she flings herself before him and cries his infamy aloud to the heavens—all men hear it—and then she stabs herself, and falls dead at his feet, and they rise up and destroy him, and burn with fire the house in which he lived. What do you think of it, Victor?"

"It's very pleasant, Howard. Write it. Mind you, I don't say that when it's published, and the young ladies go to the libraries and say, 'I want a nice love story,' the attendant will take down your book and reply: 'This is quite a nice one. Every one is asking for it. It's called *The Saint in the Sink*'—or whatever you decide to call it. I don't say that. But there's an idea behind it—and not such a fantastic one as a good many kindly folk would imagine. Any other principal characters?"

"Yes—one. The youth who loves the beautiful girl before she passes into the influence of the saint. She gives him up because she feels that his love is of earth, and is an obstacle between her and Heaven. He is young, this youth, strong and beautiful, and he loves her to the very limit of his being. He it is, in the end, who strikes the saint dead in the market-place and burns with fire the house in which he lived."

"Well, I think it's all right, Howard. It's a work of symbolism, really. I hope you'll never explain it. A symbolic writer should never explain his symbolism—it has as many explanations as he has readers. It won't be easy to write, but the fact that the idea has come to you is the proof that half the book is already written —somewhere."

"Oh, I shan't write it, Victor. What the hell have I to do with writing books? I develop the theme in my head when I can't get off to sleep, create situations, and imagine dialogue; but the next day I get up and chase Life as she speeds from me in her flying skirts—and the shorter her skirts the more ardently I pursue her."

"Yes, that's a point. Very few people want Truth—because she's naked. Therefore she attracts only the pure, and so there's not a crowd round her. But Lies, and all the hosts of Illusion, flaunt their gay underclothes shamelessly, and, if you try to get near them, you get killed in the crush. Howard, my boy, this world is the asylum of the Universe."

"Yes. And the warders are the most dangerous of all the lunatics. What the hell is that fog doing now? Lord! look at it. It looks like the devil—yawning. I shall have to stay here, Victor."

"You stay. There's nothing for breakfast, but we can share it. Your book's quite excited me. We must think of titles for it. What about *The Vengeance of the Virgin*? That would get 'em! The mere mention of the word 'virgin' has a terrible effect on some people. Besides, it's alliterative. And just think of the illustration they could put on the dust-cover! Then imagine the reviews: *Sensational—and something more*; or, *Gripping—and great*; or, *A powerful study of the eternal conflict between good and evil*; or, better still, *A first novel by a new author. We await his next work with interest*. I always like that one. I can always see the critic writing it—sitting on a fence. Oh, damn it, you must write it, Howard! You might dramatize it."

"Oh well, I'm not sure. As I see it, the curtain would have to keep coming down, Victor."

"That's all right. Let it descend. In fact, the whole of the third act might consist of nothing else but the curtain going up and down. That would be most original. You could put this note on the programme: *As it is impossible to depict the strange scenes of delirious vice enacted between the saint and the virgin, the curtain is lowered and raised again and again, as a sign to the audience that they must sit back and use their imaginations*. Nobody could object to that. It would be quite respectable. And every one would get from the third act what they brought to it. So they'd have to keep their mouths shut."

"Have you gone raving mad, Victor?"

"It's a great idea! That third act would be called *The New Realism*, or something like that. People would say it was a triumph of technical subtlety. I tell you, Howard, that third act might be the beginning of a great dramatic revival."

"Damn the drama!—I'm going to sleep."

"All right; but don't damn the drama, then. It's the greatest cure for insomnia extant."

§ 11

I remember that voices wakened me—voices heard suddenly in the great void of utter night. I remember how I started from sleep, almost in alarm, and listened intently in the darkness. . . .

"Victor!"

(The voice was a whisper.)

"Victor! are you asleep?"

(A silence—deep as the soul of night.)

"Victor! Do answer! I can't see you. It's pitch black. I must speak to you. It's—Pam."

(Silence. Then the sound of a match—a pause.)

"What are you doing there by the window, Victor? Why didn't you answer? Good Lord! have you been walking in your sleep? Don't stare at me like that, Victor; you frighten me. Say something!"

"Is it you, Pam?—really you? Or are you another vision? Ha, ha! I'm beginning to have visions."

"Don't laugh like that, Victor."

"So it is you. Your hand touches mine, and it's warm. So it is you."

"What's wrong with you, boy? You look ill. I know that I was never going to see you again, but I had to come to-night. I've been at the theatre all night. It's about three now. I had to come here. I used the key you gave me, and crept up all these dark, creaking stairs alone. Oh, this house is old—it must be awfully old! I was terrified climbing up here all alone. But I had to come—I've nowhere else to go. And now I find you here out of bed, by the window, looking as if you've seen a ghost."

"I've had a vision, Pam. I can't help laughing. I'm helpless, shaking with tempestuous laughter. My God! I've had a vision— it's going to be an interesting world if people like me who don't believe in God are beginning to see visions."

"Get back into bed; you're cold. Then you can tell me what you are talking about. You're not fit to be alone. I suppose I shan't be able to give you up, although you tire me out. You are a responsibility—I don't know what to do about you. There, that's better.

Oh, do get comfortable! Pull the clothes round you. You've no idea how to look after yourself. You're helpless as a baby. There, that's better. I'll sit here on the edge of the bed. Now, what nonsense were you telling me? You've had a dream, I suppose?"

"No, Pam. It wasn't a dream. It was real while it lasted, as real as you are. I don't remember getting out of bed. I only remember that I went to bed early. That's all. Then this dream must have come to me, and the next thing I knew was that you were calling my name and I couldn't answer. I stood listening."

"You terrified me, I know that."

"Find me a cigarette, Pam—there's a darling. There must be some. If not, we'll find some ends. Oh, you've got 'em! Sit here. I feel better now. Kiss me."

"You only had a bad dream, Victor."

"It must have been a dream. I'll tell you about it. I stood by a window—not this window. That was curious, and it wasn't this house either. It was some quite impossible building, of an enormous height. It was right in the centre of the city. I was standing by a window in a tower at the very top of the building. It was absolute night; no stars were visible, and no lights could be seen below, and yet I felt that the city was sleeping beneath me. And then I saw the prayers of men ascending to God. I *saw* them, Pam!"

"You're excited, my dear; hadn't you better go to sleep?"

"I saw them. It was incredible. Each one was a flame—a coloured flame. There were thousands and thousands of them, and each had its own individual colour. There were marvellous colours, Pam—colours for which we have no name. They were all different sizes and shapes. Some were tiny, elfish, will-o'-the-wisp flames, and here and there I saw mighty flames which were veritable pillars of fire. Some were like sparks which stabbed the darkness and died, and some were prisoned in snaky coils of smoke. Wonder turned me to stone. I *knew* that the flames were prayers. Then, as I stood gazing down, I became conscious of a great brightness overhead, and at last I looked up. The heaven was dazzling white. It looked like a dome of snow in a cathedral of ice. It was white, virgin, immaculate. And as each flame rose towards this white serenity, its individual colour fell from it, and only the soul of the flame became one with that white immensity. There, what do you think of that, Pam? It's going to be a little difficult if one is to see visions at night. Besides, there was more."

"Well, finish it. It sounds rather beautiful, Victor."

"It wasn't too pleasant to see. Well, as I stood looking at all that in amazement—suddenly it all faded. Above, below—everywhere—was night. I could not see the window against which I leant. I was afraid. Then, from far below—from an impossible distance below—I heard the sound as of a far distant sea. It welled up slowly towards me from the depths. I sought some means of escape. There was none. I was afraid of that ever-rising sea of sound. I feared that it would sweep me with it, like a leaf, towards the immensity of the unseen heavens. But I had to wait in the dark loneliness of my tower. Then, suddenly, I realized that this sea of sound was the sound of the prayers of humanity ascending from the darkness of earth. And I was afraid. But then all was lost, as the prayers swept past me, and I seemed to float up and up with them—a note in all the moving music of their flight. And above all was the over-arching silence of the heavens. Then everything died away. I was alone on the tower, and I felt a sense of immensity within me. The building, the tower, disappeared, and I stood alone, a man of immense stature, in the temple of night. I looked up. The stars were shining. And then I heard your voice calling my name and I could not speak."

"Now, you must listen to me, Victor. I've been very worried about you. Although I'd decided never to see you again, I've worried about you."

"You are a darling, Pam."

"What I've thought is this. You experience too much emotionally and mentally, because you live too much alone. You've got to get into the world of men and women. You hover above life like a bird. I think you ought to get out of this room. Although it's so central, it's remote, somehow."

"My dear, I can't leave this place. I've a great affection for it. It was here that I first brandished the torch of your beauty."

"It's all very well, Victor, but we've had some terrible rows here lately."

"Yes, I know—but I've forgiven you."

"You little beast! Every row we've ever had has been your fault.

Yes, it has—don't say a word! And the rows in which you've seemed most in the right were the very ones in which you were most in the wrong. The rows have been terrible, Victor, and that's why I left you. I couldn't bear them. When I've left you, I've often been so tired that I've felt when I've got to bed as if I had run for miles with some one flogging me. You've made me ache to the very bone. It will all have to alter, or I can't see you ever again, Victor—really I can't!"

"Where did you get those garters from? They're new."

"Oh, do be serious, Victor! You're never serious when it doesn't suit you to be. You always try to make me laugh and forget what I've got to say. You're a horrible creature, and I hate you. Moreover, I'm quite certain that you're going mad, living all alone up here, and thinking all sorts of things you don't understand. You never seem to do any work of any kind nowadays, and your clothes are awful, and, if I don't see you, you don't wash, and you won't shave; and as for ever dusting anything, well——"

"We haven't got married by any chance, have we? As I listen to you, I feel that we must be married. I know that, in former lives, I married thousands of times, and what you are saying sounds dreadfully familiar."

"I won't laugh at you—no, I won't! I hate you!"

"Now, Pam, you know, young ladies who hate a gentleman don't come alone to him in the dead of night with the obvious intention of going to sleep in his room. Not if they hate him, my dear. Really they don't. It's awfully brazen of you to come like this, Pam. I'm afraid you're a bad lot. It would have been awkward if another lady had been here."

"Another! How dare you? If I thought that——"

"But you had left me for ever, remember. After all, there are limits—even to my chastity."

"That would be just like you. If ever you do that, I'll follow you and her round the world with a dagger. I would, Victor! I know you know a lot of stupid women, who make up to you and call you a poet and flatter you. A lot of idiots! They'd loathe you if they knew you as I do. And your beastly men friends, too—pack of lunatics, who are making you a lunatic too, all of you standing on your heads till you don't know where you are!"

"I say, this is no vision—this is life all right! I'm still here!"

"Yes, and you read so many books that you're in such a muddle you don't know where the devil you are. And not content with ruining your own life, you're ruining mine. I was happy enough till I met you. Oh, I dare say you'd have called me a fool, but I don't care a damn about that."

"Oh, don't swear, Pam; it's wicked!"

"Shut up! I'm going to say what I've got to say! I was happy, do you hear, you miserable little snob! I was interested in my work, I was ambitious, I meant to get on, I had hope. Then you come along—I wish to God I'd never met you!—and you show me that everything is an illusion, that nothing is worth while, that people are all swindling swine, and so on and so on, till I feel like a shadow walking about, and every one thinks I've gone off my head. That's what you've done for me, and when I tell you about it you say it's your job to disturb people. You dare to say that to me! And when I said that I'd leave you for ever, you said that you always gave people complete freedom, and that you wouldn't try to stop me. Oh yes! and that you knew you had to learn to live alone. If I'd had anything in my hand when you said that I'd have struck you dead. There! now what have you got to say to that?"

"I think I can hear the feet of Dawn on the hills. Well, really, this has been a most charming night. I'm not a bit surprised that women were so prominent in the French Revolution. Men really have the most fantastic ideas concerning women. Who the fool was who invented the gentle, sweet, simple, retiring type of woman I really don't know. He was the world's clown anyhow. Please go on. I'm thinking of writing the story of my life, and I can put in what you've just said under the heading of 'Unsolicited Testimonials.'"

"No, but you are horrible, Victor, aren't you? Do admit it. Say that you have been horrible to me. Say it! After all, I've done everything for you that I could. It wasn't much, I suppose, but I did all I could for you, Victor. More than I've ever done for any one else. You had only to ask and I gave to you, didn't I? And then, when you made me love you, and I said I'd leave you because you made me so miserable, you said you'd let me go. I've given you all I can, Victor—I don't know what else—Victor! Victor! Don't, my dear; I love you, I love you. I came back to-night because I love you."

"Pam . . . Pam!"

"You're overwrought, my dear. You've let your nerves go all to pieces. You're getting much too thin, and you don't look nearly so well as you used to. Do you think it would be the least good going to a doctor?"

"A doctor, Pam, is usually a shadow cast by the advancing undertaker."

"Well, the truth about you is that you'll have to get yourself well. Nobody else can do it for you. The devil about you, Victor, is that you're all wrong, and yet there's something in you that's all right; but where the one ends and the other begins I don't know. Anyway, there's no good my worrying myself into my grave about you, is there?"

"I suppose, Pam, that somewhere the trees are growing out of which one day they will make our coffins. Probably at this moment the moonlight is making a silver fretwork of their branches, and the wind is stirring their beauty with an invisible caress. If ever I go really clean off my head, Pam, and die in an asylum, you might write on my tombstone: *He realized the facts of life.*"

"Why will you talk nonsense, Victor, when I want you to be practical, and take some interest in yourself—your body—for once?"

"But it isn't nonsense, Pam. It's all right merely to know things, but when you begin to *realize* them—my God! you're in for it. We *know* that the earth spins at about nineteen miles a second, and we *know* that the light from the stars, travelling at about 180,000 miles a second, takes years, to reach the earth—we *know* things like that, but we don't *realize* them."

"Look here, Victor, you're so full of theories and fancies that you don't know where you are. You must get practical. You *must.*"

"Right! I see—become a man of action. How I love that phrase! Well, what shall I do?—kill my fellow men, rob them, or deceive them? That is, shall I become a soldier, a financier, or a politician?"

"Oh, Victor, do be sensible. There is such a thing as being practical. There is, really."

"Only women are practical, Pam. Men are kids playing marbles in the shadow of the Sphinx. Women are the despair of theoretical reformers because they refuse to chase theories. Only men are deceived by the lies of the mind."

"Why do you always talk about men and women as if you are neither one nor the other?"

"Because I am neither the one nor the other. Seriously, though, I only lack one thing. Unfortunately, it's the Essential. I lack the Something that co-ordinates, and so makes organic all my thoughts and emotions. There's Something that lends perspective to all one's experiences—Something that redeems one from one's chaos. That Something is God—though I hesitate to use the word, because it is associated in one's mind with a mummy. The word 'God,' my dear, has fallen from the lips of the dead so often that, naturally enough, we associate it with death. Well, I'm not talking about the god of the dead, I'm discussing the God of the Living. One's got to find Him. First, one has to find Him somewhere, and then—everywhere. One can do nothing—absolutely and literally nothing—till then. Until then your 'man of action' is a lunatic outside an asylum. Until then, your 'thinker' is a lunatic inside an asylum. Now, Pam, I know that I fool about, jest, talk nonsense, rave, get bitter, and so on, but what I'm saying now—I *mean*. I know it's true. It's not a thing about which I argue, because one only argues to convince oneself. But I'm certain that what I've just said is true. If all the men and women in the world came to me and said, 'That's all nonsense,' I'd simply tell them to go on bowling their hoops through the midnight. Either I'll find that Something—or I won't. But until I do, I shall continue to walk blind through this world, *knowing* that I am blind, and not in the least deceived by other blind men who tell me that they can see, while I can hear them falling in the ditch. My Lord! that's a long speech. Now, you'd better jump in, little 'un; you must be tired out. Why did the fools keep you so long?"

"Oh, my dear, they're all in a most terrible muddle at the theatre. One of the principals has walked out because they won't let her have her three pet monkeys in her dressing-room."

"Well, Pam, why don't they let them sit in the stalls—with the other monkeys?"

"Ah, but that's not all. One of the authors has disappeared."

"Well, the other six will have to get on without him."

"Also, Victor, one of the backers says that unless Yum-Yum

Kickshaw plays second lead, he won't put up a bob. Well, my dear, the second lead *has* to be able to dance, and Yum-Yum can't even walk properly."

"Well, Pam, the backer will have to send his money to an Institution for Cripples instead. Muddle, mess, graft, stupidity, incompetence—everywhere! everywhere! Jump in—it's all forgotten in sleep. Lord above! What we've made of it all! Listen, here's a prayer:

"O Lord, who gavest us the glory of dawn, the miracle of day, the splendour of night; O Thou, who deckedst the spacious House of Life with infinite mirrors wherein Thy glory was reflected, so that we who enter by the Portal of Birth might find an image of Thee before we pass through the Portal of Death; O Thou, who sawest fit to share with man the spirit of creation, that out of the substance of his imagination and thought might arise the shadow of Thy glory—look now upon the profanation wrought by the hand of man; contemplate now the perversity which has distorted the perfect symmetry of Thy design; consider now the idolatry of man, so vast that all earth is become but the house of his abomination; and then, O Lord, out of the infinity of Thy mercy, destroy this travesty of Thee that usurps Thy holy places, and let all earth and its shame cease utterly and perish, so that once again the silence may ascend to Thee like a prayer."

BOOK IV

§ 1

I APPEAR again. The writing of this book is producing a curious effect on me. The book is becoming a symbol of my life. I appear and vanish in the life of Victor. If I try to write my own life, I discover that it has become merely the punctuation of Victor's life. But all that does not matter; I believe I have made a discovery.

I have spent months now turning over, reading, and re-reading the manuscript from which this book is made. I am like a spider who has visited every province of its web. I know, of course, that the web is but the spider's prison—it lives in the web, and its victims die in it; that is the only difference between them. Well, I have explored it, and I think I dimly appreciate the process by which I have been forced to the very centre of the web, where I remain stationary, brooding—waiting. The last conversation that I have just recorded gave me the clue, and I believe that for the first time I am beginning to realize something of the interior drama that is being enacted between Victor and myself—a drama that is not without its originality, if only because he is ignorant of my existence, and that I have never seen him. Fantastic as it will seem, I am certain now that one or other of us must die. I do not mean that one will do actual violence to the other—our relationship is not one which can be determined by physical means—but I am convinced that the universe is too small to contain the two of us. Either I, and all I represent, must go, or he must cease to exist. And I know that, although he is ignorant of my physical existence, I have a great effect upon his life. Yes, I know that, but I cannot explain it.

As to the revolution he has caused in my life, I can only say that the writing of this book has revealed to me, more than anything else, how complete and fundamental that revolution has been. For in this book—in what *I* have written in this book, apart entirely from those conversations which I have merely recorded—there are statements in which I do not believe, thoughts which are not mine,

and implications of a faith which is the exact opposite of everything I believe. My whole life has been undermined by this man
Victor, not so much by anything that I have actually heard him say,
but by a spirit in him which I do not understand—which he does
not understand—but which nevertheless menaces my whole being
and takes the solid ground from under my feet.

Well, I believe I have discovered a clue. I believe I know what
will determine the issue between us. If he find that Something—
God, he says it is in reality—then I know that he will leave me,
and that, without him, I shall not be able to live. Although from
the beginning I hated him, yet I have invested so **much of my**
life in him that, if suddenly it were withdrawn, I should die. And
when I say that he would leave me, I do not mean that he would
actually leave this house (though that is possible), but that, if he
remained, his very language would be such that I should not be
able to understand him.

(I have reached a point now in the writing of this book in which
I no longer care in the smallest degree whether it is regarded as
the work of a madman or not. I do not care, for two reasons: I
have seen what the *sane* people have made of the world, and I
know that what I am writing here has its equivalent in many other
lives. I know that the significance of what I have experienced is not
restricted wholly to my own life.)

If he finds that Something, I shall perish; but if he does not find
It, he will cease to exist. If he fails in his search, then my own life
will return to me. I shall get back all that I have invested in him.
I know it! I know it! I shall live again—escape—go out into the
world of men and women! I shall have done for ever with these
invisible, impenetrable barriers that separate me from Life. Ah, I
shall have done with doubts, questionings, and this ceaseless quest
of Something Else. My heart quickens, my pulse leaps, at the
thought. What madness possessed me ever to listen to the voice
of this man Victor, who—for me, at any rate—had arrived at the
limit of things, where the region of the body ends and the realm
of the spirit begins? What a fool was I! What I have missed!—what
I am missing now!

Listen. Outside, the world is a golden glory. The great beams of
the sun stream through my window, and the whole room quivers

with the heat of noonday. The familiar stir and whirl of life rise towards me from the streets below. I hear the voices of men and women, laughter, a snatch of song, cries, and all the intoxicating music of the passing caravan of life. Day after day I see it approach; day after day I watch it pass. I stand apart from it. It appears and vanishes. And I know that it is the life of this world, and I love it with the whole ardour of my being. It is the life of continual action, not the life of reflection and thought. It is a life of deeds, desires, ambitions, with definite, tangible prizes; and I know that one can lose oneself in that gay pageant and be but a note in all that brave music which thrills the unconscious hearts of the multitudes. The definite, concrete, familiar life of the world—that great freemasonry of recognized needs and recognized desires— in which doubt, reflection, or vacillation are regarded merely as synonyms for weakness; the life of acceptance—full, frank, free, and unconscious acceptance—in which desire is its own supreme justification and end. I know now that it is that life to which I belong. All else is vague as a dream, but there, there, in the world, life presents her familiar pattern—desire and strife. By day, a world of men; and when night drapes earth like a couch there is the promise in a woman's eyes.

I am like a warrior in love with war, who is condemned to watch from the narrow window of a prison cell the warlike host marching past on its way to battle. Each dawn the martial music wakes him, and with raging pulses he leaps from his bed, only to rediscover his captivity. His eyes see again the heavily barred slit of the window through which he can discern all that he is denied. Day long, he watches the moving columns, hears the familiar songs, sees the hopes written in the faces of those who march away. He shouts, he waves at the passing warriors, but they neither hear nor see, or, if they do, they glance at him in wonderment, and smile incredulously as they swing past in step with the maddening music of the ceaseless drum. Outside, beneath him, ever pass the flutter-ing banners of the hosts of life, to any one of which his heart could yield a full allegiance; but he is condemned to watch them vanish, and to spend his days in captivity, alone with his memories.

That is what has happened to me. It may happen at any moment to you. It probably will not be in the same way—but what does that matter? But suddenly it may happen that the life of this world—the life of the senses—will become unreal to you. You will no longer be satisfied with what you can touch and see. You will begin to doubt the reality of these things; you will be forced to probe, to question, to analyze. You will no longer be able to accept. The clear-cut world of desire, strife, action, will become a chaos, and you will be compelled to enter that vague, mysterious world of spirit. You will be a shadow haunting a narrow defile, on either side of which is an abyss. One abyss is the life of action, the other the life of the spirit—and both will be unreal to you. It has happened to me, it has happened to thousands, and any moment it may happen to you. Suddenly you may find yourself

> "Wandering between two worlds, one dead,
> The other powerless to be born."

But in this book I am partly concerned with the manner in which I was brought to this extremity. A wave of hatred for this man Victor sweeps over me as I sit here writing, for I know with an absolute certainty that, had he never taken the room next door, my problem would have been capable of solution in a thousand ways. After all, it was only a question under which of the countless banners of life should I march. Not a difficult problem. But now there is not a single banner beneath which I can march, and I know that, were I to fight my way through the ranks in order to march close to the symbol of the pomp and glory of the life of the world, its colours would fade, the music would die, and I should feel a ghost amid spectres. This being so, I am faced with a problem indeed. I cannot accept the life of the world, for it is become a delusion; I cannot renounce it, for all else is unreal. So I sit here—writing.

But I myself—not that side of me which has fallen under the spell of this man Victor—love the world of the senses. It is my world—I know that none other is possible for me. If I go out into the streets but seldom nowadays, it is because I envy the men and women passing through them. Yes, I envy them. I envy that easy confidence, that absolute assurance, that they possess. There is a certainty about them; they have no doubts, no misgivings. What do I care if they are ignorant and stupid? Probably ignorance and stupidity are essentials for happiness. I see them hurrying down the street, intent on their own affairs, unconscious of all else, narrowed to the moment, hurrying—hurrying. And I, who have nowhere to go, nothing to do, watch them; above all, I watch their faces, for of late I have learned to read the faces of the passers-by. The Articles of a man's actual creed are written in his face. I know the nature of the thought, for it expresses itself relentlessly in the face, and it is easy for me to conceive of a man so gifted in this study that he would have only to see a man in order to know all the inner and hidden life of that man. Even I already know much merely from looking at another—but I curse that knowledge, and all such knowledge, for I loathe that from which it is derived. It is this. To possess insight into one's fellows, to see life in any sort of perspective, it is necessary to be separated from it—to be solitary. One may be above it, or apart from it, but one must be alone. The lone wolf, if he survives, knows the habits of the pack; he understands them in a manner utterly impossible to the wolf who blindly follows the accepted leader. And he pays the price for understanding. I recognize in an instant these solitary people who are separated from life—not only do I recognize them, but I can detect the extent or degree to which they are apart. They are either silent in company, or they deliberately assert themselves in the hope of deceiving themselves by deceiving others. But the true "solitary" is usually silent, living under defences, and every social occasion is for him an affair of rapiers. He is defending himself, hiding himself, burying the secret of his solitude. This, too, I have noticed—others, who are living an active and "real" life, are anxious to label a "solitary" and dismiss him from their minds. They are conscious, in a dim way, that their activities are unreal to him, and that, were they to attempt to understand him, their activities might lose substance in their own eyes. So they dismiss him, for they know instinctively that he represents a problem which they are afraid to face. Napoleon would have been uncomfortable in the presence of a silent man who, out of the depths of a great sincerity, honestly held that Napoleon's activities were ridiculous —merely an extension of a child's game of soldiers played in a nursery. How many of us are there who are so convinced of the importance of our activities that we can dispense with the faith of others in ourselves? Very few, if any. Most of us only believe in ourselves because others believe in us. Most of us can only lead provided that others follow. We all praise freedom, but we are like birds singing in our gilded cages of the joys of liberty.

I marvel almost daily at the world's conception of what constitutes a "strong" man. A "strong" man is one, says the world, who imposes his will upon others. In the actions of others, one can see the working of his will. Good God! if the world but knew how comparatively simple it is to dominate and to fashion things *outside oneself*!—to strive, to wrestle with that which one can touch and see! All that is but an apprenticeship to Life. But that inner life—that life which is *within you*—what of that? What of the Will necessary to face that, alone, to realize it, and to seek to create a house for the soul in the realm of the invisible—what of that? To face, not men and women, but spiritual principalities and powers? To leave all the familiar certainties of the well-known highways of life, and to penetrate alone into the infinite desert that lies within you? That calls for Will of an order unguessed at by the majority of mankind. It is death and it is birth. The chrysalis is a grave for the caterpillar and a womb for the butterfly. Attempt that, and all the old solid and substantial verities become but the spectral scenery of a dream. Penetrate into that interior desert, seeking—in the words of Victor—that Something which will give perspective, meaning, and reality to all your experience, and you will learn the weakness of those whom the world calls strong.

I rebel with the whole force of my being against this thing which is come upon me. I desire this world—I love it—I long to live its life and none other. It is beautiful, rich, luxuriant. One can feel its joys quiver beneath one's hand. One can touch its fruits, and crush them against one's palate. It is warm, human, satisfying. I swear that I belong to the life of this world and to none other. Yes; the lust of the flesh, the lust of the eye, and the pride of life, I accept it all—I love it all. Surely a madness descended on me and robbed me of the sunlight, and then forced me out of the garden of life into a wilderness. But I rebel—I rebel against this spirit which denies the life of earth and leads one to spectral and icy regions. I need the human comradeship of men, I need the joy of battle with them, and I need the caresses and the love of women. I have been cheated, robbed!

Meanwhile, Time takes each day, like a thread, to weave into the pattern of the years. And I sit alone in this attic, an outcast, writing—writing. . . .

§ 2

In moments I am not deceived by the fact that I hate Victor. Hatred, like love, binds one. I am bound to him—it is enough for me to know that—and I care not whether it be hatred or love that links us together. Why, now, at this actual minute, do I not rise, leave this room, and never return to it? I have asked myself a thousand times. But the prisoner who has spent years in his dungeon learns to love it, and if one day he looks up and sees that the door is wide open, he is afraid to walk out into liberty. Once the Will has been subjected, it fears freedom. The ultimate tragedy of a life lived within the restrictions of an iron routine is that it fears the responsibility imposed by choice. To obey becomes easy; it becomes an escape, and the desire to initiate, to act, dies within one. Of all the enemies by which the soul is menaced, the most deadly is Habit. The other foes make a frontal attack, but Habit surrounds the soul. It lays siege, and its dread ally is Time. All unaware, the soul surrenders its citadel.

And I realize, despite my moments of frenzied rebellion, that I have become the slave of Habit, and that therefore I am bound by countless fetters, which are the more inviolable because they are invisible. I cannot imagine life apart from Victor. I cannot tear him out of my existence and return to the life I lived before I knew of him. No, I cannot treat him as an episode. I am involved, and his destiny will determine mine. While he searches for his Something—his God, as he calls it—I must watch, listen, and wait; but in the depths of my being I am afraid. My existence is threatened.

I had never concerned myself with questions concerning God, the meaning or purpose of life, or the question of survival and eternal life. All these were meaningless to me. I knew that such questions greatly exercised the minds of men, and I knew, of course, that most people held very dogmatic views concerning them. But such people did not impress me. I saw clearly what their lives were. I saw that their real lives were lived in complete contradiction to the tenets of their professed creeds. They believed in a god of some sort or other, either in order to conform with the lives of others, or through fear, or as a means of insurance against possible risks in the next world. I loathed such people, and I loathe them now. But they represented "religion" in my mind, and so religion for me was just a flag waved by a coward or a hypocrite, and I dismissed it as being part of the general hypocrisy practised by little people for their own mean, sordid, and dirty ends. When I encountered such adherents to a faith, I insulted them and passed on my way with a sneer. They and their gods were nothing to me. I felt no need to worship any god, for I had an interest in life which absorbed me utterly, and I knew that I had but to stretch forth my hand in order to pluck and eat of the fruit of the tree of life. That was enough for me. What else mattered? The days thronged towards me in a delirious dance, and the shadow of each as it passed was a night in which I could dream. I felt the stir in me of passions mightier than myself, and I looked around me for the means of satisfaction, realizing with joy that the attempt to satisfy was but to increase my hunger. Mentally, emotionally, physically, I was a volcano. I felt that I had burst upon the scene of life with all the strength of the depths beneath me. I questioned not this fierce desire for life—what need had I to question?—I felt it raging within me, and I went out into the highways with the determination to have and to hold—not to understand—but to have and to hold.

Why not? Around me the marvellous panorama of life was outspread. Wherever I looked there were delights that invited, pleasures that enticed, and beauties that allured. And if I gazed to the far horizon, I seemed to see a shadowy figure which beckoned me on. There was only one thing absent—and that was another with just such a zest for life as I possessed. I was drunk with the wine of life, and deep in me was a determination to *live*, to which all else was subordinated. To live!—that was my only creed. To experience all that was possible; to go to the depths if there the tang of life were keener; to seek out even suffering so that I might learn its secret. To live!—to live! I knew before I had ceased to be a boy, I knew that I had but my hour, and then all this glorious panorama would vanish into the void, and that I should know it no

more. I remember that I calculated the number of seconds I had
to live, assuming that I died at seventy—2,208,988,800 seconds!
Every clock was ticking my life away. I could hear the beats of my
own heart! Yes, I can remember more and more what I was before
Victor entered my life. To have and to hold—that was my creed;
and I despaired at the thought that to pursue one desire necessarily
involved giving up another. I longed to seize Life itself, as if she
were one's mistress, fling her on to the couch of earth, make her
mine, and then lie dead beside her through the silence of eternity.
Always, as I stretched forth my hand to take, I was haunted by the
shadows of those delights which were escaping me.

I had no need to seek a meaning to life; I had no need of God.
I felt that I was God, and I gloried in the power that I knew was in
me. And these little people round me, with their fusty little god
that they shut up all the week in an ugly church or a hideous chapel,
and visited him once every seven days to fawn on him, or to ask
him to give them all the dirty little things that their cunning had
failed to filch—what did I care about them or their god? Nothing.
I was arrogant, proud of my isolation, and I loathed their idea of
heaven with a passion of hatred. All that they condemned I loved.

So much for any consideration of God until Victor came into
my life. But then, very gradually, everything changed. The Something that Victor was seeking—and I was aware of his quest long
before he actually mentioned it—was of an entirely different order
from the outworn idols that the majority of men professed to worship. I knew that the God he was seeking was not a mere abstraction divorced from his actual experience, but, on the contrary, he
sought Something that would give all his experience a significance
and a meaning. And I knew that Victor realized that until this
Something was found he would continue to live in a chaos of
emotion, and would pass from one experience to another, finding
no relation between them, so that his life would continue to be a
series of isolated episodes. The Something which he was seeking
was a Substance that would give a reality to all the shadows which
hovered about his path. Thus it was that I saw clearly that the God
he was seeking was not the god of other men. Others, I knew,
found their lives in this world real enough without penetrating an
inch beneath the surface of things, but for Victor this world had

no meaning whatever unless he could discover the features of the Eternal beneath the masks and deceptions of Time.

In his eyes, it appeared that other men were content to bowl their hoops through the world like children, so intent on their progress that they did not see the open grave towards which they were rushing. But Victor was forced to poise any activity on the background of death, and to see whether it still maintained its shape and desirability, or whether it dwindled till it was revealed as an illusion born of vanity. This was the reason why the ambitions of other men failed to arouse in him a spirit of emulation. What were fame, wealth, genius, unless they represented something? What was beauty, unless it was the shadow of Something too glorious for our beholding? Everything had meaning—or nothing. Victor's life was balanced on that alternative, and I know that he realized that he had to find his Something, his God, for himself. He couldn't be supplied from stock. Also I know that, deep in him, Victor realized this, and was afraid of the burden of this Quest that was ever upon him, and that he sought to escape from it again and again, in the hope of finding some means of compromise that would allow him to live as other men lived. All about him were men and women who had compromised, and he saw that this compromise was made possible for them because they had divided Life up into a series of compartments, and that the activities of these different compartments were wholly unrelated. Thus their "beliefs" in no way affected their "business methods"—utter materialism walked side by side with a professed spirituality. Victor realized that these people, for all their apparent confidence, were like sleep-walkers, whose greatest fear was that they should be awakened. But he also saw that these people managed to get through the world some-how, and that they derived a kind of fictitious strength from the very fact that there were so many of them. I know that he tried to believe in them, to compromise as they had compromised, and to compete with them for the prizes which a servile world offers its greatest slaves. But he failed absolutely. Either his mask didn't fit, or he hadn't learned the trick by which, when they spoke, they concealed their opinions rather than revealed them. Or else some sudden wave of disgust swept him, and he broke every known law of etiquette and decency by saying exactly what he thought in the most forcible language possible. Whatever the reason, however, I gathered, from a thousand hints dropped by him in conversation, that he had failed lamentably in this attempt to conform. Once I overheard him say: "I can't go through life with a manicured soul, and so I'm a failure." Also I know that, above all else, he was haunted by the possibility of a life whose outward aspect would be representative of its inner truth—a life in which the Thought and Will would be revealed in every line and curve of the face and body—and he felt that the mere presence of a man who lived such a life would be more compelling than any gospel he could possibly preach. Being haunted by such a conception, Victor could not accept the lives of those round him. People seemed to him to be either marionettes or caricatures.

Each failure to conform merely brought him back to his original Quest. But he thought of another possible way of escape from his burden. There were the outcasts—those who made no attempt to conform with the standards of culture or the values of respectability. One could plunge into a life, every aspect of which revealed a complete defiance of all accepted standards. One could dissipate one's vitality in one or other of the usual ways. It was to become cynical—but why not? But the trouble was that cynicism held no secrets from Victor. He knew what it was. He understood that cynicism is merely negative faith. It proceeds from an inner rebellion so weak that it has to parade itself in order to be convinced of its own reality. Nevertheless he tried an underworld existence, but he found that he no more belonged to its pretensions than to the hypocrisy of the respectable. And so he was flung back more and more upon himself, and saw fewer and fewer people. Wherever he turned, his way was barred. He could neither accept nor compromise.

Well, and what has all that got to do with me? Why did I ever take the smallest interest in this search of his? I had my life and he had his; why did I not dismiss him as I had dismissed all others, and let him go to God or the devil in his own way? That was my normal attitude to people; why did I depart from it in this case? Once I had no answer to these questions, but now I have one, and I believe it is true.

You—whoever you are—cannot live without standards. You

have preferences, values—call them what you will. The mere fact
that you continue to live shows that you prefer life to death, for are
not a thousand means of destruction within reach of your hand?
These preferences, values, or beliefs give your life its meaning, and
the significance of your life is derived from them. They colour your
thoughts and give a shape to your imaginings. They are an inspiration to your Hope. They are the world in which you live, move,
and have your being, and all outside of them is a void. All that
you have rejected, because it clashed with your standards, lies like
a rubbish heap hidden out of sight in some corner of the garden
of your life. It may well be that you have thrown away treasures
infinitely greater than any you possess, but if, like the savage, you
prefer coloured beads made of glass to pearls, well, you will barter
even the pearl of great price for the bead of your desire. Your
preferences constitute your world. They are Reality—for you. And
the people you love are those who have the same Reality as yours.
You have "something in common," as the phrase goes. And the
people you find "disturbing" are those who deny your standards,
or those whose values include yours. You hate the former because
they deny what you affirm, and you seek to shun the latter because
you know instinctively that they are an incitement to you to leave
the limits imposed by your familiar and comfortable beliefs, and
accept the hardships of exploration and adventure. They unsettle
you. You live in your valley, which has become the world to you;
and one day you encounter a Stranger from the hills, to whom you
are drawn, and you tell him of your valley delights. He listens to
you with sympathy and understanding, and you feel that he knows
and appreciates all that you tell him better than you do; but there is
something in him which seems to say: "All this is well enough, and
it has its beauty, but over those hills there is a more spacious world,
where the sunlight is even more generous and golden, and where
the heavens blaze with a more brilliant abundance of stars. If you
leave this valley and journey to the land of which I am telling you,
it will not be to surrender anything here, for you will retain all, and
in addition discover many wonders not yet encountered." You are
thrilled with the thought that your world is not the Universe, but
soon you remember all the familiar joys of your valley, hallowed
by the usage of every day, and dignified by the traditions of Time,

and you experience a chill emptiness at the thought that you are called upon to turn your back upon all the well-defined outlines of your life, and set forth upon the hazards and hardships of the Unknown. The Pilgrim Fathers would never have sailed had they been free and living in comfortable homes. They were goaded to adventure by the sharp spur of imperative necessity. You do not wish to become unsettled, and yet this Stranger who has spoken with you cannot be dismissed. He is not a liar or a charlatan. You feel that his Reality includes yours, and you know that either you must avoid him and forget him, or leave your doll's house in the valley, and seek that realm which lies beyond the hills. His presence compels you, for it is a challenge and an inspiration to all in you that is unsatisfied.

I was the man who dwelt in the valley, and Victor was the Stranger. (One can explain second-rate parables, for the reason that they are only capable of one interpretation.) I felt that his experience included mine, and that he was the only man on earth capable of upsetting the deeply rooted faith I had in my own standards. To you Victor may seem nothing but an unbalanced, enthusiastic, and rather hysterical youth. To me he was the Stranger from the hills, who carried in his hand a mirror wherein I saw reflected a world greater than my own, and yet one in which I could trace every familiar frontier which bounded the limits of my own life. But I did not yield to him easily—in fact, I am very far from yielding to him at all, even now. But my interest was aroused from the first moment of encounter, and from the beginning I sought a means of dismissing him from my thoughts. For instance, I was always seeking a means to convict him in my own mind of a fundamental falsity in his motives, or to detect in him some mental dishonesty which would place him below even those he despised. But although, on the surface, his faults, failings, and even vices were numerous enough, yet I knew that he recognized them, magnified them if anything; and I became convinced that the thing deep in him, which was wrestling with all that sought to confine and deny its growth, was a pure thing, a real, true, and unsullied thing, and I was forced to believe in it.

I saw, then, that he was dwelling on the frontiers of my world. He was turning his back on all that I held dear, on all that in which

I believed, and was setting forth toward that realm beyond the hills which he had seen in vision, and which I had never even glimpsed. Whereas the visible and the tangible wholly satisfied me, I knew that Victor could no longer rest in them or believe in their reality, but was forced to discover the invisible and formless. And I— believing in him, as I was forced to do—was afraid that he would succeed in his Quest, for then I knew that I should be forced to go to him, to look into his eyes, and—to follow him. Yes, that is the whole truth. If he failed, the faith I had in him would return to me, and that realm beyond the hills would be but the illusion, or the lie, of a dreamer of dreams; but if he fully attained to that realm, made it his—then I knew that I, too, would catch a glimpse of that Promised Land, and would thenceforward be doomed ever to seek it, although it might well be that I should never pass through its ivory gate and find a habitation waiting for me in the midst thereof.

This is the truth of my position, and you, whoever you are who read this, may well find yourself in the same predicament. The Stranger may come to you. It is unlikely, I admit, that he will resemble Victor; but what does that matter? And if the Stranger is one who knows the ultimate secret of Life itself, he will not move you in the least—unless you are forced to believe in him. It may be against your will. But if you do believe in him, and know in the depths of you that the Reality in his life is greater than that in yours, you will be forced to seek him out; and although you run from him with the speed of light, you will discover in the end that in running from him you were but hastening towards him. Let the river wind as it will, it is but finding its shortest way to the sea.

§ 3

But it is time I left the stage. I am like a member of the audience who refuses to stay in his seat, and after each fall of the curtain appears before it and tells the spectators what he, personally, has derived from the act that has just ended. It is time I retired and allowed the dialogue to explain itself. Besides, I cannot delay. Up till now I have been concerned only with the Past, and the Present is becoming so complicated, so urgent in its demands, that I must hasten to the point at which I can record what is happening *now* between Victor and myself. I feel that a crisis is impending, and that any leisure for retrospection will soon be taken from me.

Possibly, therefore, in what I must still write in order to complete the first part of this book, it may be necessary to restrict myself, and to give simply extracts from a conversation, and to cease altogether from the attempt at realistic representation. If only I could discover a talisman that would make my selection unerring! But enough! I will resume my seat and let the curtain go up.

BOOK V

§ 1

"I HAVE one fear and one passion. The fear is—to believe a lie; the passion is—to understand. It's true, Hen! I know that I seem to be full of fears and laden with passions, but they are all superficial. Lies come to one arrayed in all the robes of truth; you have to strip them to know their essential quality. The secret of a woman's body is only revealed when she is naked. If she is beautiful, her fashionable clothes merely represent that beauty in terms of Time, but, naked, she is a figure in an eternal frieze. But one can no more strip every lie that presents itself than one can strip every woman that one meets. What's one to do, Hen?"

"A lie is a harlot, Victor; it solicits you. You can detect a lie by noting what it is in you to which it appeals. Truth makes a demand upon you. A lie offers itself—at a price. You know that as well as I do."

"I don't. I don't know anything. I keep getting glimpses of things, and then everything is lost in a void. My life is an abyss full of a white mist. Shapes writhe upward towards heaven, but a puff of wind dispels them. I'm tired of it all! I have exhausted other passions, or they have exhausted me—it doesn't matter which; but I am left with a passion to understand. I don't want to judge; I don't want to fit things into a scheme—I want to *understand*. Myself, first of all, then—others. And then—God. But how is one to understand anything, Hen? To-day one understands that two and two make four, but to-morrow two and two make five. Such are the remarkable attainments of modern science! I'm weary to death of it all! And oh, my God! how sick I am of my thoughts! The old, old thoughts that recur as often as decimals. We're given a passion for understanding, and a brain utterly inadequate to the task. But we go on trying to empty the ocean with our perforated sugar-spoon."

"You're despondent to-day, Victor. I think really the stage is your medium. You could play in *revue* one night and in *Hamlet* the next."

"Oh, shut up, Hen! The cycle of one's moods! The wheel on which one is bound! I know each mood so intimately. The mood in which one is gay—for no reason. The mood in which one is troubled about the destiny of man—for no reason. The mood in which one is concerned with the nature of God—for no reason. The mood in which one hates all men and all things—for no reason. The mood in which sexual desire seizes one and goads one on to indulgence—for no reason whatever, and despite the overwhelming evidence as to the futility of all that nonsense. Oh, and a thousand others! Yes, and the sudden, utterly irrational transitions from one mood to the other. Thus: one is walking along contemplating the joys of living like a Buddhist, without desire, when, suddenly one catches sight of a half-naked woman in a car, and immediately everything except desire is a mirage in the desert. And I'm not talking about myself only when I rave like this: I'm talking for a whole lot of people."

"All right, Victor; I didn't say you weren't. What a fellow you are!"

"Bah! how they all walk along, chattering together, keeping up the great fake! How confidently they look at you, unless you just look them quietly and steadily in the eyes—and then, my God! how their glance leaps away from yours! And yet, yet, I'm such a quintessential fool that I want to understand them, to understand them all. Why? It's all absolutely ludicrous and impossible. But there it is. We've all got some carrot or other dangling in front of our noses, and my carrot is the passion to understand."

"Well, I don't want to irritate you, Victor, and to talk platitudes. But the trouble is that sometimes platitudes are fossilized Truth. Repetition has made them fossils. If you want to understand anything, it is necessary to love it."

"Yes; I've heard you say that before."

"You sound very grim, Victor. But I'm not responsible, you know. No man ever really understood anything unless he loved it. You can't understand animals unless you love them, and you can't understand God unless you love Him."

"No, and you can't love to order."

"And you can't love to order. Precisely!"

"Well, Hen, where have we got now?"

"Where we started, of course. The end of every conversation is its beginning. It's the same with a conversation as it is with a wheel; it keeps coming back to the same point—but you've moved on a bit."

"To love them—to love them all! How impossible! It's so easy in theory. But when you see them—particularly when you see them at their pleasures—that's another thing! When you hear them laugh, when you see them drink, when you watch them eat, when you see them making love, as they call it, it is certainly not easy to love them. No, Hen, I assert, it is not easy. Do you know when I can love them, each of them, and all of them?"

"No—when?"

"When they are unhappy. I can love them—then. When they are suffering, then I can love them. I could die for them—then. Yes! for all of them. But, anyway, it's easy enough to die for any cause. What is difficult is to live for it—and to go on living for it when its leaders have sold it for a price or a photograph in the Press. That's difficult. And it's difficult to love people as they are. And most people who tell you that they love others—and keep on telling you in case you fail to find any evidence of the beautiful fact—do not love others as they are. No! most of the lovers of humanity create a fictitious humanity which they love. Such lovers are artists in their own way. They create a world of their own. And they see that it is very good. Much better than God's, in fact. And so they love it, and they are very happy, and they look very calm, and they only see what they want to see. And then—they die. And men, being flattered, put up statues to them. And then another war comes, and—with luck—a bomb destroys the statues. I'm weary of it all!—utterly, utterly weary! If I didn't see as far as I do, I'd be all right. And if I saw further—perhaps—I'd also be all right. But I can't get glasses that will make me nearly blind, and therefore happy; and I can't get glasses to enable me to read the manuscript of the starry skies. The world is a shop where every-thing is sold—except the thing you want to buy. If you ask for it, they never say, 'We'll try and get it for you,' but they regard you with a supercilious and glassy stare, indicative of silent contempt, and then say in icy tones, 'We have no demand for it. I'm sorry.'

And out you go, with murder in your heart for all the people with their noses glued to the glittering windows."

"Do you feel better after a talk like this, or worse, Victor?"

"I don't know. Worse, I think; I'm usually half in a stupor, so weary that the desire for silence, darkness, and sleep is so intense that it is almost pain. People think I love talking like this—I loathe it! I experience such a sense of degradation—afterwards—that all my body feels like living mud. But I go on doing it, just the same. I never learn. The brick wall still stands, but I've altered the shape of my head banging it against it. My head would puzzle a phrenologist, I promise you! I can understand my talking all right, but what is a permanent mystery to me is why any one listens! But they do—they do! They are all so bored—and I'm cheaper than the pictures. I commit suicide every day. We all do, of course, but I do it so violently."

"You see, your mood's changing, Victor. You're beginning to jest. You intoxicate yourself."

"It's revenge, Hen. It's a revenge on words. Yes, on words! At last I weary of trying to make them represent anything real, and so I begin to juggle with them, fling them up into the air like little, coloured, empty balls, and juggle with them, like a mountebank in a booth. No; that's a poor image! This is the fact. When I talk, I just throw the whole of my thoughts at my luckless listener. So I do when I write. Most talkers and writers just parade a select company of their thoughts, and send them out into the street of Life like demure young ladies from a highly respectable educational establishment. Out they go—the show pupils, all dressed up and walking two by two! Damn all that! Empty the classrooms of your thought and imagination. Chuck them out—dressed or undressed, dirty or clean, just as they are! Don't send out just a few of your pupils, all decked up for the occasion. No! Ring a bell—ring it damned loud so as to drown the church bells—and kick all your thoughts out of the classrooms of your mind, and let the whole lot go shouting, yelling, crying, or smiling, down the highways of life. That's the way—and don't mind appearing ridiculous, and don't care twopence if people say, 'What very untidy, unruly, and unpleasant children.' There would be some rare cripples about if people would turn out their thoughts from the schoolrooms of their minds. But there would be this advantage—the unpleasant children would die in the light, and the real ones would grow strong in the sunshine, so—three hoots for the devil and three cheers for God! And let's go out and get a drink."

"All right, madman. You're really in form today, Victor. You're all right, you know. You're better than your creed."

"That reminds me, I'm going to write out a creed. It would be a great achievement to set down in writing a creed that would not be, in reality, the grave of the faith it exists to affirm. It will be a big job. But I must really try to do it. Most creeds are but an inscription on an idol. Hark, how the wind is howling round this rickety old house! Why on earth I stay here, I don't know."

"Well, why do you?"

"I feel less a stranger in this room than in any other. And when I've climbed right up here, I do seem to have got out of it. It's like a room on the top of the Tower of Babel, and when the wind howls like this, I lie on that couch and half hope that the whole house will collapse. I think I must erect a flagstaff on the roof, and let a marvellous white banner flutter joyously at the will of each and every wind. Has there ever been a cause which mustered its adherents under a white banner?"

"I don't know, Victor. Why do you ask?"

"There is red in most of the flags of the nations, and well there may be, for there is blood on their hands. A white banner! Listen!

> The dream of a stainless cause
> 'Neath a banner wondrous, white,
> That went forth in a golden day
> And went down in an endless night.

Ah, but I believe there is such a banner, and though the cause seems to be lost, it goes on age after age. It's an invisible banner, and the hosts mustered around it are not men, but the thoughts of men, the dreams of men, the hopes of men. They lay siege to the fortresses of error, and they storm the ramparts of fortified Ignorance. Yet no blow is struck, no sword glitters in their hands, and victory is not an orgy of destruction, but a sacred opportunity for creation. No roll-call is taken in this host, and no deserter is tracked to his hiding-place. The traitor's punishment is the reward

he received for his infamy. And every Thought that rises above
the common level is a recruit. A silver trumpet calls to battle and
a golden trumpet tells of victory. The Great Crusade of the Soul
goes on, and the centuries are roads on the march. The plan of
campaign is written in the stars, and music, not dust, rises behind
the ever-advancing host. . . . There, at this moment I believe it.
Come on, let's go out. I shall deny every word of it to-morrow."

"Are you a revolutionary, Victor?"

"A revolutionary, Hen? A revolutionary? My God—yes! I want
to transform mankind and all earth. I want every grain of dust
to enter into Buddhahood. I want each one of us to cause such a
revolution in himself or herself that we arise from this mockery
of life into Life itself. Lord, man, I want such a revolution that no
man will know what Fear is!"

"Yes; I thought you probably did, Victor. I only asked in order to
get confirmation. You're very vivid to-night. I suppose you're not
writing anything nowadays?"

"No, no—nothing."

"I thought not. You're always more vivid in conversation when
you're not working."

"Sparks from a dying fire. Come on, Hen, let's go and wander
through the great city where not twelve men know their right
hands from their left. Besides, the city's marvellous at dead of
night. I love its curious nocturnal activities and, folded over all,
the great brooding wings of sleep. You wander about and, after a
while, you disbelieve in the dawn. Yes! you feel that no dawn will
ever again wake the multitudes to labour, but that by imperceptible
degrees sleep will merge into Death, and one by one every sound
will be stilled, and that Silence, like the rising tide of an invisible
sea, will cover all. Come on, let's go."

"Wait a minute, Victor. It's not too bad here. This room has
a curious effect on me. It is hung with an arras of dreams. I've
altered so since I first came here, and you, too, have altered so
amazingly."

"I haven't, Hen."

"You have, Victor; and the world, too, has altered—incon-
ceivably."

"But you say it's come to an end."

"Yes; it's come to an end. And only a handful of people know it, Victor. And when they meet each other, well, each knows that the other knows. But everything seems the same, and so you jump on your bus, pay your fare, and survey the end of the world. The majority won't believe it—although they know it—either because they're afraid, or they take the images of the old prophets too literally. We've discussed all that before. But I gather that you're not interested in the kind of revolutionary which is becoming so numerous nowadays?"

"Good Lord, no, Hen! On one side, the materialist sitting on the swag he has stolen; on the other, a looter with a burning torch in his hands; two sides of a counterfeit coin! Your possessing class with their paper wealth deny the Future, and your revolutionary class with their brandished torch deny the Past. They're the same thing, and I don't care a rap about either of them. There's a principle of growth from the seed to the flower; I'm interested in that principle in human affairs, and any one who denies it is denying the basic fact of his own life. But the goats are being separated from the sheep—thank God!"

"That's true enough, Victor. I suppose we had better go out. I can see you're restless. But what a dream that one class is any better than another, and how extraordinary to see them all getting into antagonistic little groups with their different little badges and uniforms, when, after all, every achievement of the race has been the result of co-operation. Still, come on, let's go. But I can't see you often—you keep me up all night. Aren't you taking a hat? All right. But it's blowing a hurricane. Were you ever in the illusion of believing more in one class than in another, Victor?"

"Yes—once. I thought the artists were the modern priests. But I soon discovered that most of them were only spiritual contortionists. Come on, and don't fall down the stairs. They're steep, and the whole house is dark as a tomb."

§ 2

"It's not the least use, Pam, your sitting on the edge of that chair, swinging your legs in that impertinent way, and calmly telling me that you are going away. It's absolutely ridiculous and completely impossible."

"But I've signed the contract, Victor."

"Chuck it in the fire. They won't sue you, and if they do, the Syndicate will have gone bust before the case comes up for hearing. Go away—for months! Have you taken leave of your few scattered wits? I'm the only person you know with any common sense—that's the trouble."

"Now, don't be ridiculous, Victor. I've no work—no money. You've no money, and you won't work. So I had to take this job; besides, it's not a bad part as things go."

"Now, that's a lie, Pam. There are no parts in modern drama, because there is no Whole. Nowadays, plays, at the best, are 'needy nothings trimmed in jollity.' You can't go. I need you. Let's spend the whole winter in bed, and sleep the dreary months away."

"Listen, Victor. I've got to go. I don't want to, but I've got to. And you must be sensible and do some work while I'm away and make some money. Then we'll be together in the spring, and we might go away, Victor—right away from every one and everything, right into the depths of the country—away from this absurd dusty old room, and away from the everlasting roar of this impossible town."

"Get out of hell, in fact. My dear, it would be marvellous. Wouldn't it be incredibly——"

"Oh, don't praise the idea too much, Victor, or you'll be terribly disappointed with the reality. That's the worst of telling you anything! You'll imagine a place for us to go to that never has existed and never could possibly exist—a quite impossible place where every signpost directs one to a miracle."

"Do you remember, Pam, that week-end we had in the country last year, where we couldn't sleep because of the silence?"

"You were nicer then than you've ever been. It lasted for two whole days, but you spoilt the whole thing directly you returned by becoming a complete fiend."

"Let's try to keep the conversation impersonal, my dear. But what the devil's the good of talking about next spring? The winter looms before us like a desert in hell. And you say you're going away."

"You won't really miss me, Victor. You think you will, but you won't. You'll talk yourself half dead, and then you'll sleep for two days, and then you'll talk again till you won't know which day in the week it is, or anything else."

"Nonsense, Pam. I know each day of the week intimately. Each has its own colour and its own particular perfume. But you can't go, my dear. I'm beginning to count on you more than ever. Do you know, it's a damned nuisance, of course, but I really believe I'm beginning to depend on you. And yet I really forget how we met, or when you began coming here regularly, or anything about it. But, anyway, here you are. You're a fact. I never know when you'll run in here, talking dreadful nonsense and asking for quite impossible things. But, God knows why, I like it. I like your voice, and your eyes are far apart. I even take a slight interest in your clothes."

"Well, you haven't referred to my new hat."

"That's simply because I don't want to know how much it cost."

"Well, Victor, as a matter of fact, it only cost——"

"Be quiet! I won't know! Heaven above, when I walk through the street and see the shops, how I pity men. If men could indulge their desires as easily as women, there wouldn't be a man left alive by the end of the week."

"That shows that women have more control, Victor."

"It doesn't. It shows that they desire different things. But the shops! If an inhabitant came from another world and spent a day in this town, he'd wonder where on earth the men's shops were. Of course, every now and again, you do see a kind of apologetic little shanty where men's things are sold, but on each side of it is a building as deep as hell (I refer to the Bargain Basements) and as high as Babel, with windows like glass cliffs, where everything possible and impossible for women to wear, or carry, is displayed with an artistic ostentation that is positively indecent."

"Go on, Victor; don't let me interrupt."

"And the incredible thing is that the less women wear, the more shops spring up in which the number of scanty garments is multiplied. I've a theory that, when women take the final plunge and go about naked, then the shops will get still bigger and there will be even more of them. Women will sleep in marvellous creations, and undress in the morning to go out naked in the Park."

"You do know you're mad, Victor, don't you? I mean, really and absolutely mad?"

"Hush, child! I was saying something. Already, I've heard of a woman who by the time she'd bathed, decided what clothes she would wear, been manicured, had her hair done, and so on, and so on, finished just in time to get to bed at three in the morning."

"What a liar you are, Victor!"

"It's the Age of Women, Pam. She's got everything now—except what she wants."

"And what's that?"

"It's not safe to say what it is to a woman. It makes them so furious that one's life is in danger. Men have great courage, Pam. At least, I have. I see this Age of Women descending towards me like an avalanche, and yet I know not fear. But I do confess that their shops frighten me a little. And there's this, too. Listen! Even a great drunkard can pass a shut pub. But a woman can't pass a shut shop—if the blinds are up. You'll see women at midnight, or after, gazing—ever gazing. A woman's life is a perpetual Sale in which she is perpetually sold."

"That's rather clever of you, Victor."

"Hush! don't insult me, child. Every one is clever in this age of enlightenment. There never was so much cleverness on earth. It's an age of parlour tricks; real performance is entirely out of date. Every one is clever; every one is an artist of some kind or other. To be original, you must be normal, and that, of course, is quite impossible. I've met every type of humanity except the 'average man.' He is a person we invent in order to deceive ourselves into thinking that we are exceptional people."

"Sometimes when I'm in bed, Victor, I can still hear your voice going on and on."

"Don't be rude, Pam. I'm a shepherd whose herds are thoughts, not sheep. They are always stampeding, but I can't help that. But you can't go away, Pam; it's ridiculous. I want you. I'm fond of you, confound it!"

"Now, my dear Victor, it's far too late in the day for you to pretend that you've fallen in love with me."

"One doesn't fall into love. One falls into lust. One climbs towards love. Slowly and painfully. Love is always above one, not below. Love is not an indulgence—it is a discipline. The whole of your training, the whole absurdity of education, instils into us that the art of life is to take, and then Love comes to tell us that the meaning of life is hidden from us until we learn how to give. There's a general theory knocking about that there isn't enough to go round. Men won't realize that it's their greed that creates lack, so they form the opinion that God is hard up."

"Well, I am, Victor, anyhow."

"What base ingratitude! You're wealthy   but you're not rich. You're like me in that. We're wealthy, Pam. Only the rich are poor. Any one is poor who is hungry, and the rich hunger after more money. The wealthiest man in the world is the one who lives the most. Think of the wealth of one who loves! The more he gives, the more he gets. He's in partnership with God."

"Oh, if you go on like this, I know I shall take a taxi home, and I really haven't the money."

"I'll give it you. It's not the fare that is expensive—it's the tip."

"You know, Victor, tipping is a rotten system; don't you think so?"

"We think so, Pam, because no one tips us. Tipping is oil in the machinery. It's a recognition by the individual of the inhumanity of the general system. It restores the personal element. You don't tip a number: you tip a man."

"Well, don't stop talking. I'm still here."

"Yes. But the idea that you are going away falls like a shadow between us. Do you know, Pam, that one misses a person one cares about more in a great city than anywhere else? It's true. Think how you and I have wandered together through the labyrinth of this town. And then you go, and I'm left on my own in this huge cemetery with its countless graves, haunted by the ghosts of the living. No, but seriously, you do miss any one you care about much more in hell than you would in heaven. It will be ghastly, my dear."

"But you've heaps of men friends, Victor."

"That sounds all right—but only half of me meets only half of them. Two half-men have a drink together. I'm more myself with you than with any one, Pam, because I'm not so vain with you."

"You don't mean to tell me, Victor, that you're more unbearable with others than you are with me?"

"I am, but I don't see so much of them, so they don't notice it. Besides, they're thinking of themselves all the time. You're not, and so you notice things that you've no right to. You've no vanity, Pam."

"You're the only one who thinks so. I've always heard that women are vainer than men."

"Quite. Men told you that. The vanity of man is unbelievable. Women are only vain on the surface. They are vain about their bodies, but men are vain about their souls. Even when they've lost 'em. Come and sit on my lap, Pam; I'm tired of watching you swing your legs."

"You won't like it, really. In five minutes you'll feel as if I'm cutting you in half."

"No, I shan't."

"Well, have your own way. There! Now, what are you going to talk about?"

"Kiss me. What a rounded creature you are! Don't laugh at me in that provocative way! I notice that you've nothing on, as usual."

"You've no right to notice anything of the kind. You must behave yourself. I've many most important things to say."

"You say them by your mere presence, Pam."

"Don't you try to escape like that. Listen. While I'm away, will you do some work? You're always talking, but you must write something. Will you?"

"I may. The most awful thing in the world is a nice white sheet of virgin paper on one's desk—looking at one. One sits down, and in a minute or two, that blank piece of paper looks like a photograph of one's mind."

"I don't believe you've any confidence when you are alone."

"Who has, Pam? No one. One's got to find Something so that one's never alone. I know it's true. Till then, one simply chases one sort of stimulation after another. There are a thousand forms of drunkenness. People chat a lot about the alcoholic type because it makes its devotees reel all over the place and so makes them conspicuous. But it's only one form of intoxication. In the same way, there are many more prostitutes, men and women, driving through the streets than ever there are soliciting at the street corners."

"If you remember, Victor, I just said that I had some important things to say. What are you staring at?"

"What jolly things women wear!"

"Oh, Victor! Listen to me. Now, are you listening?"

"I am listening."

"That's the first time I've ever heard you say that in my life. Oh, Lord! I've forgotten what I was going to say! You're not to laugh, Victor!"

"I'm not laughing, my dear. I am shaking with suppressed emotion."

"I so seldom get the chance to speak that I'm not surprised that I've forgotten what I had to say. It was most important. Yes, it was."

"I didn't say it wasn't, Pam."

"Yes, you did! Your body did."

"A lady doesn't refer to a gentleman's *body*, Pam!"

"Well, a gentleman usually does nothing but refer to hers. What was I going to say? This idea that women talk a lot is all nonsense."

"Quite."

"Don't speak. I want to remember what I had to say. No, it's no good; I've forgotten. You go on talking while I try to remember what it was."

"You mustn't treat me like a gramophone Pam."

"I don't, my dear; a gramophone has to be wound up. Talk about something. I want to think. Do what I tell you, like a little gentleman."

"Have you ever met a gentleman, Pam?"

"No, my dear; I'm on the stage."

"Of course, I'd forgotten. Well, I'm not on the stage, but I've never met a gentleman. I've heard a lot about them and I've seen a lot of alleged specimens, but they were simply people with good surface manners. That is, they could be extremely rude in a remarkably gracious manner. But I know there are some—somewhere. Probably they retire from the world and live in odd nooks and corners. I must go to a dealer in antiques and ask if he has any in stock. I shall probably be arrested, but that doesn't matter. Very possibly I should find my gentleman in gaol."

"I remember! Yes, it's this. Do you know, I had a feeling that it was right for me to go away and to leave you. Yes, that's it! That's the real reason why I'm going."

"Well, I'm damned!"

"Not quite—but very nearly. I don't know what made me feel this, but it came to me—suddenly. Something is going to happen, and I know that I mustn't see you for a while. I'm certain of it, Victor."

"What's going to happen?"

"I don't know. Something is going to happen to you. I know I was thinking that you couldn't go on for ever like this, and then I suddenly knew for certain that something new was going to happen to you."

"I know! I'm going to die! Hooray! I'm going to die! I'll send you a wire from the next world: *Arrived safely; pleasant journey; rooms quite comfortable; writing; love.—*Victor."

"Idiot! Of course you're not going to die. I can't explain anything, but I know I've got to leave you for a time. You count on me too much in the wrong way for the wrong things. You get your own way in everything, and it's desperately bad for you."

"If you decide to marry me at any time, you will let me know, won't you? I must have a little notice."

"You're not at all the type for me to marry, Victor. I've thought over all that."

"You have!—when?"

"Oh, often—when you've been talking. Yes, I've thought that over thoroughly. But you're not the sort of person to see every day. You are like a baby, and if I married you I should have to start right at the beginning and teach you everything."

"Teach *me*, child?"

"Yes, you, baby—everything. You haven't got into this world at all yet. You're a firework. At least, people can dismiss you as being only a firework. And that won't do. You mustn't let people be able to dismiss you, Victor. If you'd only pull yourself together, they would find something in you that they couldn't dismiss, and it would do them good to run up against it."

"*You're* the firework, Pam, and a most dangerous kind. Always going off when you haven't been lit."

"Shut up! I'm talking."

"I've told you before that you mustn't say 'Shut up!' to people."

"I don't—to people. I do to you, otherwise I'd never get a word in. Well, that's the real reason I'm going away. Of course, I want the money and all that, but it's not the chief reason for going. But it's all going to be no good, Victor, if you're simply going on in the same way when I've gone. What you've got to do is to take stock of what you are, see where you stand, recognize what your job is, and start right in on it. I know that there is a job for you, and one that only you can do. I'm sick of seeing the best people chuck themselves away."

"What do you mean by that, Pam—exactly?"

"Never ask me what I mean *exactly*. I'm never exact, boy. But I see it at the theatre and everywhere else. The best people, and by 'best' I mean the most alive——"

"That's a good definition, Pam."

"Don't interrupt. The best people nowadays are the most muddled, the most disturbed. It's difficult to explain what I mean. They don't seem to know what to do with their vitality. They've seen through so many things that deceive the majority, and yet they've not found anything to put their money on, so to speak. Well, in the end, in a kind of desperation, they fling themselves into something to which they don't belong. Dorrie, a girl at the theatre, did that. She was a marvellous creature. Quite a child, really, with the face of an angel. I've never known any one with such a love of life as Dorrie. But she was in a devil of a muddle—didn't know what to do with herself. She really loathed all the rubbish and tinsel of a stage life. But there it was, all round her, flattering her, inviting her. Well, suddenly, she flung herself into it. And what a welcome she got from all the dreary, half-dead people who give parties and go in for all sorts of filth and rubbish to try to convince themselves that they're alive! That crowd know instinctively that they can only keep their fake going by getting hold of people like Dorrie. They're a lot of vampires living on the vitality of others."

"Well, what happened, Pam?"

"Oh well, as Dorrie couldn't live in a sewer, it did her in. You see, she went into it headlong. The vampire crowd don't do that. They look after themselves. They're careful, and are well preserved—

like mummies. But Dorrie wasn't like that. She couldn't turn her life into small change and then bet in half-crowns. She staked all she had—and lost. And that's what happens to so many of the best people nowadays. They chuck their lives away in the service of a cause which they loathe. It's not good enough, Victor."

"No, as you say, it's not good enough."

"Why, without the Dorries of this world, that crowd of parasites couldn't go on. They've no life of their own. They exist on the vitality of others, and destroy them, in the process. I'm sick to death of seeing it go on all round me. It's time the people who are alive realized themselves and stopped wasting themselves."

"By God, you're right, Pam!"

"I know I'm right. You look at their faces and you see what Dorrie looked like when she first came to the theatre, and you'll know by that how the thing works. It's time it stopped."

"Yes—it's time the dead buried the dead."

"Dorrie was an obvious case, Victor. But I'm certain that the same thing goes on everywhere. It may not be so easy to see, but it's there. These parasite people *seem* to be powerful, influential, and all that. But it's a fake—nothing else—they're just dead, and they live on youth. They deceive, and if you yield to them, they never leave you alone till you're one of them. Then, of course, you've joined the great conspiracy and you go on like them."

"'No man might buy or sell, save he that had the mark of the beast.' It's true, Pam, every word of it."

"Well, my dear, you've been taken in by subtler forms of the same thing."

"You mean that the idol has a thousand faces, each covered with a different mask?"

"I scarcely know what I do mean, Victor, but I know I'm right. It all came to me with a rush. I can't quite make out what's happened to you. You've been guarded in some way."

"Guarded!"

"Yes; if you'd had your own way, the idol—as you call it—would have got you all right. But Something has guarded you. You've not been allowed to chuck yourself away. Don't you get conceited about it—it's all been done in spite of you."

"Now, don't let's be rude to each other. Go on."

"Well, my dear, your nurse is leaving, and you've got to get out of the nursery and go into the world. You think you've finished. You haven't—you're just going to begin."

"Oh, Lord, Pam!"

"You are—you're going to begin. You're the most fortunate person I've ever known."

"You're sure that you're not muddling me up with some one else?"

"Certain. You—Victor—that's who I'm talking about. You know all sorts of things; you've a power in you, and you're just frittering it all away. It's wanted, down there, in those streets. You've got to go into the world, boy. And I'd say all this if I knew that it meant that I'd never see you again. And that would hurt—a lot. I'm very fond of you, although you're often quite horrible to me."

"Now, don't introduce a new theme. I don't know that I like anything you are saying too much. It makes me feel as if I had a responsibility."

"I should just think you have a responsibility! I like that! You've been shielded the whole of your life. You're in debt for that—for every minute of it."

"I don't want to hurry you away—but are you sure you won't be late? The time's going on."

"You idle, good-for-nothing little beast! You know the truth of what I've said. But you're lazy—lazy! My God! I've never known anything like it! You just want to dream—to read and to dream. But that's all over. You'll either go out into life of your own free will, or be kicked out into it."

"Good Lord, Pam! You make me feel like a conscript in wartime."

"It's going to be war. It is war—out there in the world. Not the usual kind—it's—it's——"

"Spiritual war."

"Yes—that's it. Call it anything you like. All this came to me with a rush. I didn't understand it. I saw it—suddenly. I say! I must be too heavy for you."

"No, don't move. I don't think I can let you go away. All our relations up to now seem to have been a kind of preliminary. I don't know what I mean, but I mean something. Anyway, you're right in this—I'm at the end of my tether. There's no doubt about that. Things can't go on with me as they are. But then, if you come to that, they can't go on as they are anywhere. Do you know, there's going to be a hell of an upheaval soon, and it won't be caused by any of the things that people will say are responsible for it! The apparent reason for it won't be the real one. Its true origin will be deeper than their deepest guess. And the type of people who are making that upheaval a certainty are the very ones who think they can prevent it. But they're in a hell of a funk all the same. Their sham, surface honesty shows that. Still, it's a privilege to be alive in this age."

"Well, you realize that, Victor. It's probably true. But idle dreaming is no good."

"You mean that one's beliefs must be tried and tested on the field of life. Perhaps you're right. Perhaps the time has come when one has got to make one's beliefs one's daily bread. I don't know, but I have thought about all this lately. Fools, knaves, and parasites have usurped the world too long."

"Well, I don't understand much, Victor, but I've got eyes and can see what is going on all round me. And I'm sick and tired to death of seeing the real people just chucking themselves away, trying to grasp a shadow which they don't want. They get hypnotized somehow. They seem to think that because so many other people want certain things so badly that—somehow—those things must be worth having. So they go out to get them, knowing all the time that they don't want them. I might have done the same if it hadn't been for you."

"For me!"

"Yes—you. You opened my eyes, and you've opened them so wide that I'm beginning to see your faults."

"I must take you to an oculist, my dear."

"Idiot! There, now, I will kiss your eyes. One—two! And now, really, I ought to go. There! are you crushed to death?"

"Crushed—rubbish! I'll carry you round the room."

"Oh no, Victor! Put me down! Put me down! What a lunatic you are! You'll only tire yourself."

"There—now, what shall I do with you? I'll put you in this chair. That's it. Now—when are you coming here again?"

"Never! You've disarranged all my clothes. What a nuisance you are! Well, perhaps I will come again—soon."

"Come for the night, and we'll discuss everything. And then you'll go away, and God alone knows what will happen."

"It will be all right, Victor—it will, really. I must go now. Kiss me."

"Good-bye; bless you."

"Good-bye."

THE PRESENT

BOOK I

§ I

I HAVE been ill for some time, and am still far from well. I have spent my days and my nights lying on the couch. Every book that I have attempted to read has fallen from my hand, and I have known a weariness of body and an emptiness of mind which have made each hour an eternity. I have seen no one except the landlord, who brought me what little food I required, and for some ridiculous reason I dreaded his visits far more than being alone. It is terrible to be with a person, even for a few minutes, with whom one is in no relations of any kind, and it is worse when the person in question is not a stranger, in the strict sense of the word. This landlord of mine, for instance, is no stranger to me in one sense, for, after all, I have lived in his house for years, paid him rent each week, and exchanged a word or two with him nearly every day of my life; and yet I know nothing whatever of him, and he is entirely ignorant of me. The fact that we have spent years near each other has no significance whatever. Any two men passing each other in the street below are not more apart than we are. One thing, however, I think I have discovered about him since I have been ill, and that is, that he dislikes me in a vague sort of way, though I am convinced that he has never formulated the reason for this aversion even in his own mind. Also, I have an uneasy kind of feeling that he wishes me to leave this room. Why he dislikes me I have not the slightest idea, but I am pretty certain I am right, and the fact disturbs me very much indeed. One thing, however, I did notice: the landlord stared at me intently when he thought that my attention was not concerned with him, and also I fancied that he did not understand certain of the remarks I addressed to him. But, anyway, I greatly preferred my solitude to his presence.

During my illness I came to the decision that I had reached the point at which I must cease the attempt to give in this book any further account of my past relations with Victor. This is why I am now beginning the second part of this work and am concerned with the Present. But I would not have any one who reads this imagine that I decided not to continue to write of the Past because I had exhausted my material, or because I considered what I have written to be in any degree adequate. I must emphasize that I have not employed the hundredth part of the material available, and am far from satisfied with what I have written.

One thing more I must say here. Although I am about to write the second part of this book, which is headed "The Present," it must be understood that in it I am concerned with recent events. In the first part of this book, as I have already stated, I do not know when the happenings recorded occurred. I cannot even guess. Some time within the last few years is the nearest I can place them, and it must not even be taken for granted that their order is chronological. But with this second part I do know that I am concerned with the past few months. But why do I try to make clear that which is chaos? This nonsense about Time wearies me. Everything happens at every moment, and the attempt to describe a process or development in terms of time is ridiculous. It is of no importance *when* an event occurs. Life is to be measured not by duration but by intensity.

§ 2

It's no use trying to deceive myself. It was fear that made me ill—fear of the silence. That sounds absurd, but it is true. In the early stages of my illness I said to myself, again and again, that Victor must have gone away. But just when I had convinced myself that this was true, I would suddenly hear his voice and, to make matters worse, I was convinced that he was alone. I know from my own experience how easily a man living in a room alone falls into the habit of talking to himself. But for some reason it frightened me to hear his voice. It was worse than the silence, and it was terrible to me to think that here were we two, so near to each other, alone each in his room, separated only by a wall. And then the obvious fact occurred to me, that he must know perfectly well that I lived next to him. Of course he knew! He must have known from the beginning. But what was I to him? Just some man who lodged next door. (We are all so apt to think that those in whom we are deeply interested are also interested in us.) He would have overheard no conversation in this room. How long is it since any one came to see me? I forget, but it must be a long time. Years, I suppose. But, anyway, what would he care about me? I half think that the landlord believes that if I don't move from here it doesn't matter, as I probably shall not live long.

But why the silence next door? Although it is true that people have been to see him during these last few months, yet visitors have been rare; and I know that he has been in there, next door, alone. Can it be that he is working? I wonder. I do not know. And this sudden breaking forth into speech—what is the meaning of it? Is he talking to himself? And, above all, why is it that I do not understand certain of the things he says? He might as well speak in a foreign tongue, and yet I know that they have a meaning, and unless I can discover their meaning, I shall lose Victor as completely as if he left this house for ever.

When I first began to write this book, it gave me a curious type of relief. The fact that I was dealing with the Past was an escape from the problems of the Present; but now the writing of this narrative is painful to me. I am like a man with nothing to leave who is making his will. I only continue to write through habit, for although this work seems a short one, for every page that I have retained I have destroyed ten that I have written. . . . I prop the pillows behind me, rest the manuscript book on my knees, and write.

I always leave the curtains open, day and night. I like to see the pageant of the day. Sometimes I wake suddenly to find that dawn is looking in through the window. It is as if some one stands outside, who is looking at me in an impersonal way, without any curiosity whatever. Then I note how the day grows to the full stature of noon, and dwindles gradually until the first hints of dusk creep imperceptibly into the room, and with them come unhappy and faded thoughts into my mind. Dusk is the autumn of the day. It is beautiful, but hopes that seemed so real in the morning flutter sadly down from the turrets of the mind, and the bleak empire of night opens out before one. Then, one by one, I see the coming of the stars, and sometimes a yellow moon rides proudly like some great galleon through the dusky ocean of the skies. And as the night waxes, so the sounds of the street grow less, until all the world seems to collaborate with the silence of these two rooms, where two men dwell alone with their dreams.

The hours move slowly through this room in a solemn procession, like mourners at a funeral. Their hands are empty, and each is so like the other that they seem like nuns wending their way through the cloisters of Time. And yet, long ago—years ago—did not the hours dance past me like gay revellers in fancy dress, hastening to shower confetti in the mad whirl of the Carnival of Life? And Victor? What do the hours bring to him? I ask—and only the silence answers me.

I know perfectly well that I stand on the threshold of a crisis. I have known it for several weeks past. But until this actual minute, I have refused to recognize it. I suppose a murderer sitting in his cell the night before his execution manages, somehow, not to believe in the inevitable. One refuses to realize certain things, and yet, at the same time, one realizes them absolutely. But to-night I am forced to face the fact that a change of a fundamental nature is about to occur. I know that a blow is to be struck, but I do not know where my enemy lurks nor the weapon with which he will strike. But he is on his way towards me—silently, relentlessly. And I am afraid. I know that it is completely impossible for me to continue like this. I know that were it to be so, I should die, and yet I fear change with the whole of my being. Yes, I am afraid. And I know, too, that in this silence my destiny is being determined. I am in the dock, and next door sit the judge and the jury trying me for my life—in silence. It is incredible, ridiculous, fantastic, but it is true. I look at the pile of manuscript of this book which lies beside me, and a fear passes over me that in it I have written a full confession of my guilt.

Guilt!—the word is like a stab from an invisible dagger. I feel guilty. I feel that I have wronged thousands, thousands of unknown men and women, and—worst of all—I feel that I have wronged the unborn. I have wronged them because I have robbed them. But of

what? Of what? Lately I have striven with all the power within me
to remember all the incidents of my life. I have summoned events
from the uttermost recesses of my memory that I may judge as to
whom, or what, I have wronged. I find nothing that could not be
found in the life of any and every man walking along in the street
below. I say this, and I know that I am honest in this statement, and
yet I feel as guilty as though I knew of some great crime committed by me for which I must make atonement in suffering. Surely
this is madness that has come upon me. Do men drift into madness
slowly, by imperceptible degrees? I feel a thief—not as the world
uses the word, but in some deep, terrible sense. I have stolen an
invisible essence; I have stolen Life itself and claimed it as mine.
I feel as if I had been entrusted to guard some holy house, full of
perfect possessions, but that as soon as I was alone I flung wide the
doors, and invited coarse and drunken revellers to enter as guests,
and make free with the treasures that were not mine, and hold
delirious orgies of cruelty and vice in the inner sanctuary of the
house. And now the revellers have left me, and I am alone, amid
the ruin and wreck of all the calm and beautiful serenities that
once lent peace and spacious wisdom to the glory of this house.
Yes, I am alone, amid the havoc and the shame; and I know that
the owner of this fair mansion is on his way towards me, and that
in his hand there is an inventory.

But, side by side with this sense of guilt, there is a flaming, angry
Thing within me that seeks arrogantly to justify itself, and to deny
with hatred and scorn all that dares to criticize or to judge it. This
Thing of flame within me ransacks my memory, and gloats with
feverish delight over the faded scenes of pleasure and debauchery
which it discovers in the dim depths of the Past. The anger of this
Thing within me grows as it gloats, and the memory of its old
triumphs feeds the flame of its hunger for new conquests. At times
it rages within me like an imprisoned beast, and then it turns into
a snake and glides among my thoughts, infecting them with its
venom, till all my mind is but a writhing Medusa of desire. It can
assume all shapes, all disguises. It creeps, like a spy, unobserved
into the fortress of my Will, opens secret gates to the host of its
invisible allies, captures the citadel, and plans enormities as it feasts
on the spoils of victory.

And then suddenly, for no apparent reason, a great sense of peace pervades my whole being, and I experience a freedom and tranquillity for which there is no name.

Such is my life as I lie here on this couch, and I smile when I remember that I thought, when I first came to this room, that I had a problem to solve that demanded immediate solution. The irony of it! My life then was a lake ruffled by the gentle breezes of summer. Now it is a tempestuous sea, lashed by a screaming wind, a tempest in which, now and again, comes a sudden calm, when the ocean is like a mirror, above which flash the celestial hosts of the stars.

But enough of this! I am weary, utterly weary of it all. I am concerned with Victor—only with him.

The last few months have furnished only one coherent conversation. I will give it here, for, apart from it, there are but monologues and fragments.

BOOK II

§ I

"WE'RE great idiots to say good-bye in this room, Victor. We ought to have left each other in the street."

"Oh, it's better here, Pam. Besides, you can't say good-bye in the street. We should simply get knocked in different directions if we paused for a second on the pavement. Men have filled the world with machines and now spend their days scampering out of their way like frightened mice—and they spend their nights lying awake because of the infernal roar of their inventions. Listen to it now! Everything is shaking—the room, the town, the whole world! And for what? So that people can fly from one place which they loathe to another which they detest, in order to do some work which they abominate. What a triumph!"

"I don't like leaving you, my dear."

"It's probably right, Pam. You deliver me from boredom, and I suppose one has got to get to the other side of boredom. One appears to have to get to the other side of most things. What awaits one when one is the other side of all things, God alone knows."

"But you get bored in a more terrible way than any one else, Victor."

"Don't you believe it, my dear. Boredom is the greatest product of civilization. I shiver when I hear people talk about boredom in a light way. I'm convinced that crime attracts a lot of people simply because it appears to be exciting. It's the same with vice, and that is why people get so furious when they discover that vice is dull. My dear, believe me when I say that what is called the love of adventure is really only the fear of boredom. Men rush into war because they imagine that, whatever else it may be, it won't be dull. Nowadays, they are disappointed because modern war is monotonous, like everything else. It has been captured by the factory system. No, boredom is like every other horror—there's no way round it. There may be a way through it. Perhaps I'll find it while you're away."

"I'm depressed about everything, Victor. I don't want to go, I don't want to leave you, and I've an uneasy sort of feeling that something is going to happen while I'm away. It must be all nonsense. After all, you've plenty of people to see, haven't you?"

"Too many—many too many. I know quite well that, if I wish it, I needn't spend an hour alone. It's awful. It's a terrible indictment of life that people want to see me. That fact alone tells you all that you need to know about the kind of existence that these people lead. Well, Pam, I'm not going to see them—not any of them."

"Why not?"

"I'm going to be alone and see what happens. I've spent a hell of a lot of time alone, God knows, but I'm really going to live alone while you are away. Talking is an escape—it's a way round. Well, I'm going to find a way through everything that is keeping me out of my own. I've a place to find and a work to do, and a thousand things are keeping me out of that place and away from that work, and I'm going to go clean through the lot and take what is mine with both hands. And you can only do that alone. No one can do it for you."

"But you're not going to spend all your time alone in this room, Victor, are you? You must go out and you must see some people. For Heaven's sake, don't go from one extreme to the other! You always seem to me to leap from the edge of an abyss to the verge of a precipice. You're not fit to be alone; that's the trouble."

"I wonder if I'll believe that you exist—when you're gone."

"I don't know what on earth you're talking about, Victor."

"The world is absolutely a different place for me in every way when I'm alone. All the things that most people find solid and substantial become the most vague and unreal to me when I am alone. I have ached with loneliness in my day, and yet, I've always known that one has to find Something that will redeem one eternally from the possibility of loneliness. But I won't talk about it—or anything. I will fold you in my arms. I will wrap you about me, close my eyes, until I know that we are not two, but dream that we are one, and that no shadow of separation can fall between us here or hereafter."

"Victor . . . Victor!"

"Pam! . . ."

"It's dusk, boy. I can see the stars through the window."

"All day I have been leaning out of the window, Pam, watching the leaves flutter down. One is never conscious of the trees in this town until the autumn, and then one discovers them. One learns more of people and things when they bid one farewell than when one first meets them. When one first meets them, one wonders what they are going to give; but when they leave one, one realizes what they are taking away. The year is dying and you are going away."

"And yet, Victor, really, we've been very unhappy together, haven't we?"

"Terribly, my dear. That is why we shall suffer so in separation. We shall realize that all the awful rows we've had were but the breaking of those barriers which prevented a true meeting between us. People who have been merely happy together don't miss each other much. They soon become merely happy with some one else. One can always find a dancing partner. A trifler can always find a dish to suit him on the menu. Listen:

> "Into the Restaurant of Life I came,
> I chose a table, and I took a seat,
> The orchestra caressed a theme of flame—
> A waiter paused to see what I would eat.
> I scanned the long, expensive bill of fare,
> Designed to satisfy my every wish,
> I must confess that everything was there,
> Except the thing I craved—a simple dish.
> I asked the waiter. 'Non, Monsieur,' he said.
> 'Prepare it, then!' I cried; 'I'll sit and wait.'
> He looked at me as though he wished me dead,
> Repeated: 'Non, Monsieur'—and flicked a plate.
> 'Send me the maître d'hôtel!' He ambled up,
> All wreathed in confidence, and smiles, and fat;
> But when I told him how I wished to sup,
> He went death-white: 'We're never asked for that.'
> So I had nothing, just sat on until
> The lights went dim, then rose—and paid the bill."

"When did you write that, Victor?"

"I went out to dine with a man at one of those huge restaurants

—you know the kind—vulgarity aping dignity. Well, he crossed to another table to talk with some friends, so I spent the time writing that stuff on the back of the menu. Anyway, I had a poor evening. Never mind that. I'm serious enough, though, when I say that we shall miss each other because we've been unhappy together. That's true enough. I don't believe you are going, Pam. It's a dream—in a dream."

"Don't let's talk about it. Let's enjoy ourselves and then, suddenly, in the middle of it all, I'll get up and run away."

"Like Cinderella? Well, perhaps you're right. Anyway, what I feel about your going away can't be said. You've been away often enough before, but this time it's different. Oh, I know we shall meet again all right, but I don't believe it will be in this room, somehow. Don't let's talk about it. Don't let's talk about anything. Lie close to me, enfold me, and let this great bubble of a world burst!"

"Do you remember that you once told me that one doesn't fall into love, but that one climbs towards it?"

"Yes, I remember, Pam."

"Well, it's true."

"Everything I say is true. Don't you dare to laugh! Yes, everything I say is right, and everything I do is wrong. Apart from that minor discrepancy, my life is entirely consistent. I can scarcely see you any longer. I can only hear you laughing in the darkness. We're strange lovers, you and I."

"Why strange, Victor?"

"Strange, my dear—strange. Where the love of most people ends, ours began. Where the road ends, the road begins. I had a dream the other night—I'd forgotten it till this minute. It was twilight, and I stood in a great mountainous ring which was the meeting-place of all the roads in the world. I cannot describe the scenery, but it was completely unfamiliar; it was unlike anything I had ever seen before anywhere. Every road in the world led to this place, and down each road came multitudes of people. As each person arrived in this circular space, he or she was disturbed to find that there was no road leading out of it. Every one was in a great state of bewilderment, and each was asking the other where to find the continuation of the road down which he had travelled.

But there was no road out of this strange and twilit place. I noticed that new arrivals were, at first, excited and pleased at the novelty of their situation, but that, very shortly, they became irritable and then frightened. Also I saw that many made determined efforts to retrace their steps along the road that had led them to this place, and I saw them fighting their way back along a road down which fresh multitudes were ever advancing. And I noticed that, although they appeared to make some progress, the throng of new arrivals was too strong for them to contend with, and they were carried back to the circular place where all roads end. Every one argued with his neighbour as to the direction to take in order to escape from this unfamiliar place. I noticed one in the throng who told them that the circular space was surrounded by mountains and that they would have to climb. He told them that they would find the tracks of climbers who had gone before, and that they would leave a track for those who would follow them. But they cried to him: '*Show us a road!—a road that we can see!*' Each one shouted: '*A road! a road!*' till the tumult became deafening and I awoke."

"You told me once, Victor, that you never dreamt, and now you seem to do nothing else. I don't believe you dream these things at all. I believe you make them up and tell them to people. You always were an awful liar!"

"There's not much difference between the things we dream and those we imagine, Pam. And if all life has become to me as the semblance of a huge dream, then am I not as one who walks in his sleep, and is not every word I utter but the shadow of a dream? Soon I shall lie here in the darkness alone, and I am afraid that then you, too, will be as a dream."

"Oh, Victor, I wish we hadn't come here tonight! We ought to have gone to a show. Any show would have done."

"Oh yes! Any would have done, because they're all the same. That's true enough. If you visit the serious drama, you are shown mental underclothes; and if you go to the frivolous drama, you are shown actual underclothes. It's an age of lingerie. No, my dear, it's better here in this room. The curtain of night falls upon the stage of the world, and Silence broods above the vast auditorium. I shall remember this night when you are away. I shall need to remember it."

"I shall write to you often, Victor. I shan't say anything in my letters, because I can't express myself in writing. Directly I sit down to write I find that I have nothing whatever to say, or, if I have, I have no words in which to express it."

"You seem to me to possess every qualification for a popular novelist. No—that's cheap. I'm not serious. It doesn't matter what you write. God knows what I shall write to you, but that doesn't matter either. Soon, the only art that will appeal to us will be music. The symbols of all the other arts are derived from the furniture of this world. And this world is over. But music is different. It represents a higher experience and, therefore, it employs purer symbols in its manifestation. No, I'm glad we are here to-night. But I shan't come to see you off to-morrow. A railway station is as dreary as a Materialist—it's simply mechanical arrival and departure. It makes me imagine what birth and death would be like if there weren't God. A railway station, in theory, is the triumph of Time. Everything is balanced on a minute. Thank Heaven, the machinery breaks down and everything is always late! Otherwise, Time would be triumphant. As it is, a journey gives one an excellent idea of Eternity."

"How you rattle on!"

"Whistling to keep my courage up. Whenever I hear any one jesting, whenever I hear any one laughing, I always wonder what they are like when they are alone. That tells you nothing about others, but a good deal about me. My dear, how the time goes! I can hear the seconds pattering like rain. It's awful. And your family awaits you!"

"Yes. And they don't even know of your existence, Victor."

"The world knows nothing of its greatest men, Pam. That they know nothing of my existence does not worry me. What does—is that they exist at all. That sounds rude, but it isn't."

"I'm glad you told me. I might not have guessed."

"Still, I suppose it's natural that they want you to sleep at home to-night as you go away for some months to-morrow. . . . Say something! Can't you see that I'm trying to be broad-minded?"

"I don't want to go home, but I shall have to. Why does one find a family so difficult, Victor?"

"Because a family so often represents a term of imprisonment without the option of a fine. You've got to know people in a true way in order to live with them. Many families are just a collection of strangers who know each other's habits. It isn't enough. People loathe their relatives because they feel that really they are expected to like them, and as they know, instinctively, that you cannot compel affection, they rebel against a false convention that demands an impossibility. But the minutes fall from us like fine sand. Don't let's talk about anything."

"I shall miss you terribly, Victor. I'm more alive when I am with you than when I'm with other people. Other people seem to have stopped growing. They are all fixed and finished, and they all seem satisfied with themselves."

"Pam, my dear, if all I have ever said is a lie, here is a truth: there's no sin like self-satisfaction. It is cancer of the soul. It eats its own substance and imagines that it is being fed."

"You unsettle me, you tire me, you make me hate you sometimes—but you do make me feel alive. I'd forgive you anything—because of that. I'd do anything you asked me—because of that. And I have done everything you've ever asked me, including all sorts of things that I never should have done, haven't I?"

"Everything, Pam."

"Well, that was the reason. And it's not going to be easy for me away from you, but I shall have a good deal to do, so it won't be so bad for me. But when I return, we shall have to stop living like this and talking the nights away. If we're really fond of each other, we must find a work to do together—something that only we can do. That's true, isn't it?"

"It's true."

"And you'll think over all this when you're here alone, and when I come back you'll tell me all your plans?"

"All of them, Pam."

"And you won't make an idiot of yourself, or go melancholy mad or anything, will you?"

"No."

"I can't see you at all now. It must be getting awfully late, Victor."

"It always is. I saw an inscription on a sundial once which read: *It is later than you think.* I used to give that as an answer to people who asked me the time, but I gave up doing so, as I found that my popularity did not increase. And I saw quoted in a poem the other day that a man had said that he didn't like sundials because they always strike sooner or later."

"We're going to the country together next year, Victor?"

"Yes, into the depths of the country—where one can hear the echo of one's own thoughts."

"We deserve to go, my dear; we've earned it. Doesn't that sound absurd when most people are always going to the country?"

"No, Pam, they don't go. They take the town with them. They go to the country either to murder things, or to continue that slow process of suicide which they have decided to call Life. Don't talk about others. I'm trying to love them, and I succeed when I don't think about them."

"I shall have to go, boy; light a candle."

"Kiss me, here in the darkness. Bless you! I can hear your heart beating. My God! What a queer business it all is—beating hearts—breathing lungs—bodies—thoughts—desires—hopes—days—nights—weeks—years—Life—Death! It's beyond me—it's too much for me! Too many miracles! And yet people walk about with dragging feet, and look at the world through lack-lustre eyes! I'm certain that, if all the dead leapt from their graves with a mighty shout, most people would say, 'There, now! Well, I never! Nice goings on! What's the Government going to do about *this*, I should like to know!' I'm finished, I'm over! I'm lost in a labyrinth of miracles. I don't know where this world ends and the next begins. Here's the candle—and there's the light. I'm coming down with you, Pam. I can't sit here and listen to the sound of your departing feet. Ah, I forgot! You are going on a journey. I will kiss your feet. There—there!"

"You're a mad creature. Kiss my lips . . . my eyes. . . . There, now take my hand and we'll go down together. Oh, my dear, we have been happy here! It wasn't fair to say that we had been unhappy."

"It is over, and we see now that we were happy, because we were together. Come! I met a ghost on these stairs the other night, and he bowed to me most politely. That made me think. There! Out goes the candle! . . . down we go together through the darkness. . . ."

BOOK III

§ 1

I HAVE made a discovery: Victor is writing a book. I am certain that this is so, and this fact accounts for the silence in the next room. Yes, he is writing a book, and every now and again he pauses in his labours and reads aloud some passage he has written. There is no other explanation. So here I remain, on the very threshold of Victor's life, collecting fragmentary reports of the state of the conflict within him. For I know that the book he is writing is not a book in the ordinary sense of the word, but that in it he is battling with Something in himself, and that the whole of his life is in issue.

A change, therefore, has entered into my relations with Victor, and it is fundamental in its nature. Until the past few weeks, I have only heard Victor when he was with others—and how many of us are entirely ourselves when we have an audience? There is a wide difference between hearing what a man says and listening to his most intimate thoughts. These past few weeks I have been listening to Victor's thoughts. I have been an eavesdropper, not merely on the threshold of his room, but on the threshold of his soul. But I feel no shame; I only feel hatred and a desperation so fierce in its intensity that I know that soon, against my will, I shall be roused to action.

I break off to curse this silence. The hours move slowly towards me, slowly pass me, like the dead in their shrouds groping their way to the next world. I have lost the sense of my own individuality and am numbed by the silence. Delusions possess me, and often I feel that I have died and am awaiting I know not what in some dim corridor in the next world. It is only that I fall to sleep and dream, I suppose, but I find a difficulty in determining when I am awake, thinking my own thoughts, and when my mind is captured by some phantom born of a dream. Also I am conscious of darkness all round me, covering me, and this consciousness remains even when I see plainly that the sunlight is streaming into my room

and turning even the dust into a shimmer of dancing gold. I seem
to be outside myself, watching myself, dispassionately, and with a
strange indifference to my destiny. Even the thought that perhaps
in truth I am seriously ill and about to die does not move me in
any definite way. I watch myself on a stage, and I know that if
the curtain falls, it will rise again—if not in this world, then in
another. I am not interested. Once I was vitally interested in the
life of this world. That life is over, since it holds me no longer,
and any other type of existence will only be a continuation of the
ghostly life which I now lead, and—I am not interested. I know
that there is a life after this one, but to me that is merely to say that
the play which is boring me has another act. Very well. Let the
curtain fall when it will and rise again when it must. I am not to
be deceived by a change of scene. The characters will be the same,
however greatly their costumes may alter. It is all mummery and
nonsense, and not for one single second can it give me the illusion
of reality. Let it go on, and let the fools applaud, weep, or hiss, as
they choose; it is nothing to me how they respond to this senseless
juggling with a threadbare plot. If I could believe in death, I might
be able to believe in life; but I don't believe in either—I can't believe
in either. Life is an entrance into one labyrinth, and death is an exit
out of that one and an entrance into another. That is all, and does
it matter to me in which one I get lost?

A great contempt for men and women has entered deep into
me. I am outside them, and I see so clearly how they are fooled.
They are pitiable creatures. They are so easily cheated. I see them
with their eyes shining with joy or blurred by tears, and their happiness and their sorrow seem to me to be equally meaningless.
But, above all, I find their ambitions ridiculous. I see them climbing to the turrets of the ruined House of Life in order to throw
themselves down on the stones below. For a moment they stand
poised high above the throng, and the plaudits of the mob rise
towards them, and then they grow giddy and fall, and their place
is taken by another madman intoxicated with the illusion of his
own importance.

Most of all, though, I loathe in men and women that damned
conspiracy to pretend that life is worth the living, and that death is
some short cut to an eternity of unimaginable felicity. They are so

in love with their miserable little desires that they convince themselves that somewhere Reality will coincide with their wishes. If not in this world, then in the next, but Somewhere—Somewhere —it must be so. So intensely do they want it to be true that it *is* true—Somewhere. The conspiracy! the conspiracy! I see it everywhere. Fools! The donkey with the carrot held in front of his nose believes that he has only to walk far enough and it will be his. So he walks till he drops dead, and all the other donkeys say: "He had only to go a bit farther and he'd have got it, but, anyway, *he's got it now.*" I have seen the truth—the truth is that we are cheated, and to find any happiness you must be able to deceive yourself and find a carrot to lure you on to the grave—and another one to deceive you in the next world. Give the carrot any name you like—I don't care. I'm not impressed. Call it Love, Ambition, Hope, the Meaning of Life, God—anything you like. It's just a carrot, but it will serve as long as it is just beyond your reach. Strain every muscle to reach it, but pray that you may always fail. If you make it yours, you will not desire it; you will throw it away, and seek another—but, remember, the stock of carrots is limited. Remember, one carrot is needed for every fool. So be advised in time, for when you cannot find another, your life will be like mine, and you will cease to be deceived by the great conspiracy. At that moment your life will be over, and you will hover like a shadow on the outskirts of the multitude. But, at first, you will thrill with pride at having passed beyond the illusions that hold your fellow-men. You will regard yourself as free in a world of slaves. You will be proud of having discovered the Truth—yes, you will spell it with a capital T—and you will imagine that now you have power, and that now you will be able to take your place in the world. Then you will make a discovery. You will find that you still have a carrot—your carrot will be that you haven't a carrot! You will possess a metaphysical carrot! And then the final discovery will dawn upon you; and that is that you cannot live without a positive carrot. Yes, you will find that you can only live if you believe in an illusion, and that to have seen through all the illusions will not provide you with a way of life.

These are my thoughts as I sit here alone in the silence, and then suddenly I hear Victor's voice. He has paused in his writing and reads aloud some passage he has written. Listen!

There is no search but the search for the Supreme Being. I do not use the word "God," for that word has been robbed of meaning. God has been made the perquisite of the priest. They have buried Him in sepulchres of stone and in sepulchres of speech. Endless repetition has rendered His name meaningless. They have banished Life from their lives. They have perpetrated the greatest crime of idolatry—they have created an invisible idol. Who shall arise mighty enough to destroy this invisible idol before which humanity is prostrate?

I must summon all the forces of my mind that, when I think of God, I hold in vision all the infinity of starry heaven, the Silence that enfolds the mountains, all the majestic beauty of the unfathomed sea, and, above all, my thought must penetrate to that profundity that lies hidden in the heart of man, of which he is afraid, and by which he lives, grows, and feels all that which lies above, beyond, and below the limitations of speech. I must hold this vision when I think of God, otherwise I shall but wander through this vast cemetery of a world, where every grave contains a murdered thought of God.

In just this manner does the voice of Victor break the web of my thought, and when all is silent again I sit here disturbed, and am unable to collect my interrupted speculations. And it is most remarkable that, whenever his voice breaks the silence to read a passage from the book upon which he is at work, every word that I hear him say is in absolute contradiction to what I am thinking. So unfailingly is this the case that sometimes I feel convinced that he is aware of what I am thinking, and that he selects a passage to read aloud which is a complete repudiation of everything that I am convincing myself is true. But of course that is all nonsense. He knows nothing of me, and would care nothing if he knew me. He is going his road and I am going mine. He is separated from me by a thousand barriers.

How we delude ourselves! How we torture ourselves! We are all alone—utterly alone. The distance that separates the most remote star from this planet is no greater than the distance between two human beings. We all dream of some other person so near to us that the pattern and colour that life presents to us will be shared by that other human being with a perfection of sympathy and understanding. So certain are we of the possibility of such a communion that we seek everywhere to find this other one whose mere presence would make us complete, and end the tragedy of the isolated and divided beings that we know ourselves to be. We haste from one person to another—seeking, seeking. We are so certain that each newcomer is the one for whom we are searching that we blind our eyes to all evidence to the contrary, until proof too overwhelming to be overlooked presents itself, and then we turn away with hatred in our hearts for the innocent being who, we sincerely believe, has deceived us. We are alone, and those who seem nearer to us are in reality most removed. I am a complete stranger to Victor, but I am as near to him as any one else will ever be. But not one of us faces any of the facts of life, for each fact makes happiness impossible, and at any price we are determined to be happy.

If I die to-night (and it's quite possible) and arrive shortly afterwards in the dreariness of another world, and am asked by disconsolate spirits for my impression of life on this earth, I shall say to them that the chief characteristic of mankind is hypocrisy. The first game that we play as children always begins, "Let's pretend," and we continue the game of pretence to the end of our lives. But we soon cease to be honest enough to say, "Let's pretend," so we say that what we want to believe is true—*is* true. We believe what we hope. We lie about everything—our virtues, our vices, our hopes, our dreams, and our desires. And by God! we are satisfied with ourselves, and we judge others, and wrap ourselves round with a cloak of hypocrisy till it becomes as much a part of us as our very skin. My life opens before me, and I see that in the space of a few brief years I have passed from a passionate love of life to a bitter and complete renunciation of life. I can scarcely believe that when I first came to this attic I was so full of the zest of living that I did not know to which activity to turn for fear of limiting the experience that might be mine. What a fool! What a dreamer! Is one life any different from another? Strip any life you will of its external trappings, and you will find the same starved creature shivering beneath them. Beggar or millionaire, harlot or hero—what does it matter if you penetrate beneath the surface? Walk in purple, or go in rags, as you will, we are beggars all. Yes, mountebanks or charlatans, plying our thievish little trades or performing our swindling little tricks on the great highway of life. Oh, it's a brave and gallant company!—if only you can deceive yourself. Only deceive yourself, and you will find a welcome and fine companions to travel with along the glittering road. But fling from you all that you know is counterfeit, renounce the false, and refuse to serve a lie, and you'll soon find yourself alone in the gutter splashed by the mud of the passing squalor that seemed so gay when you marched in its midst.

I know well enough what label people would use in order to dismiss me from their lives—they would call me "bitter." But it may be that Truth is bitter, as bitter as death, and that it is a cup that all must drink sooner or later—in this world, or the next, or the one after that. We live a lie, our lives collapse, and we say, "An enemy hath done this thing." So we live another lie—with the same result. Well, when you have sickened of the cloying sweetness of lies, you will turn with eagerness to the bitter waters of Truth. As I sit here, ill, weary, depressed, knowing not what the morrow holds, and fearing the dreams of the darkness, I swear that I would not exchange all this wretchedness for the happiness that is born of a lie.

I see no people now. I know that I have only to be seen to be hated and despised, but I am utterly indifferent, for I understand others, and I know why they hate me; and I also know that I am an enigma to them—something that must be dismissed and forgotten. I am the grinning skull at the feast. The revellers do not know why the skull grins, but the skull, in its day, sat at the feast and knows the end of folly. But I am no better than the rest of the fools. I am worse. For I am still proud. If I were not, would I trouble to write this? I am alone, an outcast from life, and the last deception—Pride—enters my empty heart and keeps me company.

But why am I so terribly excited, and why is my whole being in an agony of expectation? Suspense stretches me on her rack, and I know with a terrifying certainty that Change stands outside my closed door with a hand raised to knock. Or is the figure that I know stands without the figure of Death? Could I possibly be so excited about dying? Am I really so childish as that? Bah—to the devil with Death! I am dead already, and the figure outside my door is probably the undertaker. I derive comfort from the reflection that I shall never be able to pay him for his services, and that he won't be able to writ me in the next world. At least, I hope not. You never know, though. I expect there are spiritual capitalists in the next world.

§ 2

I am wakened from sleep by the sound of his voice. I feel that it is very late, but I remember that there is no significance in that, for he often sits up most of the night working. Why am I forced to listen? Why do I not stop my ears? Am I always to be haunted by the sound of his voice?

Out of the chaos of my spirit emerge moments that I do not understand, but which make the rest of my life an impossibility. In these moments I am no longer a single, isolated being, but am part of a vast invisible structure that I feel is without limits, and is not susceptible to the perpetual pilferings of Time and Change. These moments are not some sudden ecstasy that leaves me exhausted and irritable. In them my identity becomes merged in something infinitely greater than myself. All irrelevancies fall from me, and I am strong with a strength that is not mine. I am raised above Life, and I see it outstretched beneath me in a never-ending perspective of beauty. I love with a love of which I am normally utterly incapable, and I desire to possess nothing in the whole universe, but to give to all out of the infinite wealth of this love that is not mine and yet which is mine to give.

I am no longer a separate note, but am become a part of a majestic symphony which fills all earth and heaven.

But these moments are rare. They become but a memory, and I cease to believe in them, and explain them away to myself. But it always happens that when I have finally convinced myself that they possess no fundamental significance, again I am raised above the level of my normal existence, and a sense of serenity enters me so overwhelming in its calm certainty that doubts and misgivings become ridiculous, and I know that these moments are true and that the rest of my life is false.

One can live in the wilderness until one has caught a glimpse of the Promised Land. Until one has had a vision of the Promised Land, one does not realize that the wilderness is a wilderness.

§ 3

Some old philosopher said, thousands of years ago, that one could know the whole of life without leaving one's room. It is natural that I should believe that the statement is true. When the squirrel ceases to run round his revolving cage, he discovers his captivity. I look out of my window and watch the hurrying crowds in the street below, and I feel that I, who have had no experience as the world uses the word, have in fact experienced far more than the majority of men. They have only been concerned with what lies outside them, whereas I have always been at desperate grips with that which lies within.

I am determined not to yield my own personality wholly to the influence of this man Victor without one last struggle. I feel like a defender of a fortress, most of which has already passed into the hands of the enemy, but one tower of which is left; and I am determined to barricade myself within it and to defend it with all the weapons that I have not yet surrendered. I have determined to exert the whole force of my will against this influence which is robbing me of my own personality, and I will continue to hold to my own thoughts, to cling to them with all the strength I possess, and to dismiss these ideas of Victor's which conflict at every point with the purpose and meaning of my own life. What is he to me—with his visions, dreams, and illusions? This house is a prison in which an invisible fetter binds me to an invisible man. . . .

My landlord came into the room this morning. I was writing at the time, but on seeing him I put my pen down, and made some ridiculous remark about the weather. (Why is it that we *dare* not be silent with a stranger?) He answered me, and seemed to want to talk, which is very rare with him, and suddenly a feeling of exasperation came over me at the thought that we had never exchanged a single confidence of any kind, or, indeed, expressed one of our real thoughts. He was still hanging about, so I said to him:

"What do you think of Life?"

He looked at me, saw that the question was asked seriously, and replied:

"I haven't much time to think about it." (He is a little man with a bald head, and is continually fidgeting with his rather ugly hands, which bear the marks of years of toil.)

"No," he repeated; "I haven't much time to think about life. By the time I've got through my work, and done all the things I have to do, I'm glad enough to go to bed. There's a lot of things I'm always saying to myself that I will do when I have the time, but the days pass, and I usually discover that I don't want to do any of them." He laughed contentedly. "You cease to want a thing if you have to wait long enough for it."

"Would you live your life over again?"

He looked at me in a bewildered sort of way.

"I've never thought of that."

"But would you?" I insisted.

He paused for several seconds. "No," he replied. "I wouldn't live it over again. Once is enough for most things."

But I wasn't satisfied. "Is there any day you would live over again in its entirety?"

He looked at me rather suspiciously, I thought, and did not answer for a moment.

"I don't think so," he said. "Would you?"

His question took me completely by surprise—why, I don't know. I have no idea for how long I was silent.

"No," I answered; "not an hour of it."

"That's all very well," he said, "but you don't want to die, do you?"

He spoke in a most matter-of-fact, everyday way, and yet somehow I felt that I was becoming the witness and he the cross-examiner.

"I don't think I care much whether I die," I answered.

"Oh yes, you do," he said. "We all say a lot of hard things about life, but we don't want to die." He paused. "Just before you came here, my wife died." He spoke without any trace of emotion. "Well, I thought that night that I wanted to die more than any-thing else, but gradually I remembered that there were a whole lot of things she'd want me to do, so I thought I'd do them first and then die afterwards." He broke off and smiled. (His whole face changed in an instant when he smiled.) "Well, I started to do those things, but I haven't finished them yet, and I expect I'll leave a lot of them undone when I do go. You have to go on—that's all about it."

"But why—why?"

"You have to—that's why. There's no good asking questions. You do what you have to do—and that's all about it."

"But supposing there's nothing you want to do?" I objected.

"Then you have to do what you don't want to do. But you can't do nothing. If you don't work—like you—you have to think. If you do work—like me—you haven't time to think." He paused, then added, "There's a lot of talk that every one ought to work nowadays. Well, I'm peculiar, I dare say, but I'd rather work than think—any day. I've only thought about twice in my life, and I didn't care about it much."

There was a silence. Then he went on:

"I thought a bit when my wife died, but it didn't get me any-where. I didn't understand her death then, and I don't now, for that matter. Then I started on the work nearest my hand, and everything seemed to fall into its place."

He paused again, and then added inconsequently, "I used to be in the Army."

"God!" I replied. "I should hate that like hell."

"You wouldn't," he answered. "They were the happiest days of my life. I didn't know why I was happy when I was in the Army, but I do now. It's a simple life—that's why I was happy. You do what you're told. That's all. Just do what you're told. If you do that, you have no responsibility whatever. If you don't do it, there's the devil to pay! You know where you are. It's a great life."

"It's my idea of hell."

"You're wrong. Once you can choose for yourself, you don't know where you are. When I came out of the Army, it all seemed strange. There didn't seem to be any rules. You could do what you liked, so, usually, you made a fool of yourself. I believe that's why I married."

"So as to be under orders again?"

He laughed, and in an instant seemed quite young and attractive.

"Maybe you're right. Anyway, a woman often does know what she wants—they can all say what they like to the contrary. I didn't know what I wanted when I came out of the Army. But I'm wasting your time chattering about myself."

He looked at my books and papers, and I discovered from the expression in his eyes that he was the only grown man I have ever met who had the smallest respect for a student.

"You're not wasting my time," I said. "I've nothing to do, really. I write and read simply from habit. Books, to me, are a kind of mental pub." He said nothing, and I saw that he didn't understand.

"Well," he said, preparing to go, "it's nice to have a bit of a chat sometimes. Makes you feel more alive, somehow."

"Have you ever been into battle?" I asked him.

"Yes, several times." He paused. "The funny thing about it is that when I'm awake I can't really remember much about it—only noise, dirt, and cries. But I dream about it sometimes, and see things that I know happened to me. Clear as daylight I see them in dreams. But when I'm awake it's all confused. Not that I ever think about it. It's just a thing that happened—that's all." He paused. "You know, it isn't my fault that your room is in such a state. You're here so much that no one can get in to keep it clean. I've often meant to explain that."

"That's all right," I said. "I like dust. It reminds me of the destiny that awaits me, and it keeps me humble."

He laughed. "You're like my wife. She used to say to me, 'Everything gets to the dust-bin, sooner or later.' She used to say some queer things sometimes. Your saying that reminded me. A queer woman, she was. It's a funny thing to say, but in a way I'm blessed if I don't understand her better since she's gone than when she was here. Every now and again, when I'm thinking about nothing, something she once said to me comes into my mind, and I think, 'So that's what she meant.' It's strange, but there it is. It doesn't do to think about things too much. That's what I say, and I stick to it."

"Do you ever read?" I asked.

"I can't get on much with books," he answered. "It's a question of getting used to them, I suppose, like everything else. My wife used to read a bit. She'd read to me sometimes. But I couldn't make much of it. Now there's a funny thing to do—to write a book! Fancy sitting down to write a book!"

"Why do you think that's funny?"

"Because I do. For one thing, fancy having all that in your head! It's not natural, somehow. But I'm ignorant. I know that. You mustn't take any notice of me. Books are necessary, or they wouldn't be written."

I smiled. "Do you think that everything that exists is necessary?"

"Of course it is," he answered, "else it wouldn't be there. That's clear, to my way of thinking. Once you get away from that, there's no sense left in anything."

"Well," I said, "I envy you. You're a happy man."

He looked at me quickly to see if I was joking, but when he saw that I wasn't he looked puzzled

"You've got me there," he said. "I've never thought about that. 'Pon my word, now I come to think of it, I don't know whether I'm happy or not. I don't believe I've ever asked myself the question."

"Then you've answered it without asking it," I said. "Unhappy people, like happy people, don't ask the question either—but it's for a different reason."

"That's too deep for me. You find some queer things in those books of yours, I dare say. Still, they are company for you. You spend a lot of time alone. Well, I suppose I must get on, though, as I was saying, it's pleasant to have a chat now and again, just to find out you've still a tongue left in your head. Not that a rare lot of time isn't wasted in chattering, because it is. But, in reason, a bit of a talk sometimes does you good."

He shuffled round the room a bit, made one or two remarks, and disappeared. I heard him going slowly down the stairs.

Directly he had gone, I felt a strong inclination to call him back and to question him concerning Victor, but immediately I realized that I could not discuss Victor with him or anybody. What was remarkable was that, directly my landlord had left me, I felt a sense of peace and, for the first time perhaps for years, I had no hatred in my heart for Victor, but a sense of pity for him, for myself, and for all men.

§ 4

I alternate between a feeling of fierce superiority over other people and a conviction that every one in the whole world is better than I am. The latter mood was created in me by my conversation with the landlord, and I criticized myself with a bitterness that surprised me. I felt that I was worse than those I despised, and that I was below all that which seemed beneath me.

How inadequate, feeble, and futile are books! I know that there are emotions, thoughts, convictions in this landlord of mine greater, more profound, than any that find expression in books. He is unaware of them, of those thoughts and emotions, but what does that signify? How real he seemed in his simplicity! how human and unaffected! And yet he is precisely the type that, in the abstract, I should dismiss entirely as being "the average man." Of course, it is one's pride that dismisses him in this fashion, for, underneath, one knows that to understand the average man is to discover how closely one resembles him. Anyway, after the conversation I have had with my landlord, our relations can never be what they were. Even if for years I never speak with him again, except to say "good morning" or "good night," still, we have met—we know each other. And why is it that in true conversation what is said is so supremely unimportant? Perhaps this is the real explanation of the fact that with those most intimate we are silent. All pretentious conversation is like the wind—it disturbs the surface of the lake, and thereby mars the beauty of that which its tranquillity reflects.

How one contradicts oneself! The statement that one wrote yesterday, believing it to represent all that one holds for Truth, becomes, to-day, not only a lie, but a lie which one repudiates with the whole of one's being. The mind creates labyrinth after labyrinth in which to lose itself. How we deceive ourselves! How we torture ourselves! We are afraid of the simplicity within us, for it is deceived by nothing, and it bids us assume the responsibility for everything.

§ 5

I am restless to-day, ill at ease, and antagonistic. Of all moods that possess me, this is the one that I loathe the most. It usually swoops down upon me during the most hideous hours of the day—from two till five in the afternoon. Nothing has shape, nothing has colour, nothing has purpose. All exists unto itself and for itself—a world of mute and passionless warfare. Those things seem truest which, normally, one denies most passionately. A gaunt, obvious world.

I know that, if I had less vitality, this mood could not visit me. I know that, if I had more, I should rise above it. As it is, I can neither read, nor sleep, nor walk through the dull and chilly streets that seem to stare reproachfully at the skies. I write this merely to escape from thoughts that stand at the threshold of my mind inviting me to entertain the spectres of desire. I am weary of the three-card trick of Passion.

Why is it that just when I have forgotten Victor, he always gives me a sudden reminder of his existence by reading aloud some passage of the book he is writing? To teach me, I suppose, that there is no escape; that I am a prisoner in an unlocked room—the most abject of all captives. All the doors of the prison of Passion are unlocked, for those under sentence therein have forged their own fetters.

This is what I am forced to hear:

For months, or it may be years, I have striven to discover by what sign I shall know that I have escaped from bondage. I think I have discovered it. I shall know that I am free when the commonplace no longer exists for me. Yes, it is as simple as that.

Realizing that, I begin to understand what the commonplace is, and why it is a menace to the growth and development of the soul. I see now clearly that I am truly living only when I am stirred by the spirit of wonder. I realize that only then do I respond to all the miraculous life that leaps within me, and become one with all the beauty that surrounds me on every side. And it was the realization of this which revealed that the everyday acceptance of a large part of one's experience as commonplace is the blinding of oneself to half the beauty of life. I see that, until all things become new to me, I am still in bondage. The issue is clear: at every moment one must be born, or at each moment one dies a little.

But I recognize that, like everything that one has to do, this is impossible. That I, who have known weariness and a boredom seemingly limitless in extent, have now to strive till I reach that level upon which negative emotion is not possible, is simply fantastic and ridiculous. But the only alternative is to continue to deny those moments which visit me, and which give all Life its significance and meaning. To continue to live like that is to deny the highest in me, and not to continue to live like that involves the endeavour to raise the whole of my life on to another level.

The extent to which we regard life as being a commonplace affair is an exact index of the mechanical nature of our own existence, for the "commonplace" is all that which we have allowed to die beneath our eyes and, therefore, it represents all that which we have to raise from the dead. The spirit of wonder performs this miracle. All things are subject to it, for all things were fashioned by it.

His voice dies away into the silence, and I am alone again with my thoughts. I hear what he says, I set it out here in this book, but I do not understand half its meaning, and each of his utterances is more obscure to me than the last.

Am I really awake as I sit here writing? or is all this, and all these past years, but a dream from which I shall soon awake, to find myself again in that familiar and comfortable world which I once loved with so passionate an ardour?

Ah, if only once again, be it but for an hour, I could crush the maddening lips of Life against mine in the frenzy of a desperate kiss! For there was a time when she yielded to me with a perfect acquiescence. And now—now she is dead, and I cannot find where they have buried her. Often I have sought her grave, but I knew that my search was vain, for in truth my heart is the sepulchre where she lies dead.

§ 6

Again I hear him reading aloud.

Two dreams visited me last night, and all this grey wintry day they have been more real to me than the familiar spectacle of everyday life.

I was asleep on my couch when suddenly I became aware of a radiance flooding a corner of my room. There stood a woman, whose beauty was not of this earth; and gradually I realized that the light which surrounded her was an emanation from her own naked loveliness. She was robed only in the light of her own beauty, and silence, like the soul of music, hovered about her.

I opened my eyes, and she vanished. I closed them, and again I saw her. With eyes closed, I stretched out my arms to her—and again she vanished. I lay still in the darkness with closed eyes, and again I saw her, resplendent in the quivering light of her own beauty. I spoke to her—and she disappeared. I besought her to return, but only the darkness answered me. I prayed to her that she should tell me her name—only her name. The sound of my voice died away. I was alone. In my despair, I said to myself, "I am unworthy of her." And again she stood before me like a living flame. And I awoke.

I do not know how long I lay awake in the darkness, or what I thought about the dream I had had. But again I slept, and again I dreamed a dream.

I found myself in a kind of cell, and in it a man was seated. There was a great nobility in his face, and immediately I knew that he was unaware of my presence, and I also knew that he was a saint. I was amazed to discover that I could see what he was thinking, and that I knew everything concerning his life.

And I saw what was troubling the whole of his mind, and it was this. He loved all things in heaven and earth with a love that passed understanding, but one person he was unable to love, though he strove to love her with the whole of his strength. He could not love her—he loathed her, for she seemed the denial of everything that filled his soul with rapture. And I saw the face of this woman whom he loathed, and everything within me froze at the hideous horror of her ugliness. It was nameless in its obscenity. So I stood in the cell with the saint, knowing what was torturing him, and I pitied him.

Then suddenly another appeared in our midst. He was a man of extraordinary beauty, and I could scarcely look upon him because of the glory that was his. The saint rose and stood before him, and the stranger said, "Come." And immediately everything disappeared, and the three of us seemed to be sinking down through some dark immensity of space. And I knew no fear, and was surprised that I was not afraid.

Then the three of us passed together through some dark corridor where bats flitted past us, and we walked in silence. There was an odour of death and the sound of cries and wailing. We entered a room of indescribable squalor, and on a foul couch lay the woman whose ugliness had chilled my being. She lay asleep, revealed by a fitful beam of light cast by a haggard and dying moon.

The saint stepped back with an exclamation of horror, and the hatred that he felt in his soul for this woman made his face terrible to look upon. Then the Stranger bade him go near to her, and he seemed forced to obey. I approached her with him, and the terror of her ugliness entered into us. I heard the voice of the Stranger bidding the saint to look yet closer into the face of the sleeping woman, and I, too, gazed upon her intently. Hours seemed to pass as we stood there. Then the Stranger asked the saint what he saw, and he replied that it was as if there were a mask upon her face, and the Stranger bade him remove it. With a trembling hand the saint removed the mask, and the face remained terrible in its ugliness. Then I saw that beneath the mask that had been removed, there seemed to be another, and I heard the voice of the Stranger bid the saint remove this also. It was removed, and then another, and another, and another. I stood fascinated, for, as mask after mask was removed, the face of the sleeping woman grew less terrible, and at length she appeared human as she lay there asleep in the light of the moon. The saint paused and looked at the Stranger, and the eyes of the saint were wet with tears. But the Stranger commanded him to continue his task, and mask after mask was removed, till the woman was beautiful with a beauty mighty enough to bring all the peoples of the earth to her feet. And again the saint paused, and again the Stranger commanded him to continue. Soon the beauty of the woman transcended the beauty of earth, and the saint was afraid, and cast himself on his knees before the Stranger and besought him that he might go back to his own place, for he was afraid to look upon the glory of the sleeping woman. But the Stranger commanded him to continue, and the hands of the saint trembled, though his face became radiant as if a light shone behind it. All the room was filled with splendour, and the beauty of the sleeping woman became more and more transcendent, so that I almost feared to look upon her. Then the saint gave a great cry, and prayed the Stranger that he might return to his cell, for he feared to look upon the face of God. But he commanded him to remove the last mask, and behold, the room was as a lit temple, and the woman lay in all the unimaginable splendour of naked wisdom, and she opened her eyes, and I saw that she was the woman who had appeared to me in my first dream. And I awoke.

§ 7

One final episode, and I must pass to the narration of that which is seething within me. . . .

I woke suddenly last night to find that some one was in my room. The figure held a lighted candle in its hand, and for one impossible moment I thought it was Victor. Then, to my amazement, I saw that it was my landlord, and at the same minute he spoke to me.

"Are you ill?"

"No—why?" I answered.

"Then you must have cried out in your sleep several times. I heard you shouting, and so I came up."

I lit the candle by my bed and stared at him in astonishment. He was in a dressing-gown, and I saw that in one hand he held a glass.

"I've brought you some brandy," he added.

I lit a cigarette and then said to him:

"It couldn't have been I."

"It must have been," he retorted. "I expect you've had a nightmare. Here, drink this."

"All right, I'll drink it, as you were decent enough to bring it." There was a silence, then he said:

"You're spending too much time alone, if you ask me. It's all very well studying and all that, but you can do too much of it. Besides, you don't eat enough. You ought to go out a bit and enjoy yourself. Not that it's my business. I know that. But I'm beginning to feel a bit responsible. Why don't you go out and amuse yourself?"

"I can't find anything that amuses me—outside."

"Well, you know best, but I've been a bit worried about you lately. You don't look as well as you used to."

"I'm all right," I said. It was difficult for me to speak, because I felt a great affection for this man who, until a few days ago, had been a complete stranger to me. Again there was silence between us, and every now and again the wind wailed about the house and then died away.

"It's a rough night," he said. "It's the kind of night that, when you lie in bed listening to the wind, you don't feel as if you were in a town at all."

"Yes," I replied. "I know what you mean. You feel that if you looked out of the window, you'd see a tumbling sea, raging with anger, under the moon. I know. I've often thought that."

"One thinks queer things at night when one can't sleep. It happens seldom enough to me, thank God! but it does happen sometimes. I'll be glad enough when the morning comes. You aren't cold, are you? It's bitter to-night."

"No, I'm not cold. But I'm not like you—I don't want the morning to come. I like lying here listening to that wind and thinking of the sea. That's better than the everlasting sound of that damned traffic."

"Well, I'm glad you are not ill, anyway. But if you care to stay in bed to-morrow, I'll get you anything you want."

"You're much too good to me," I said.

"One must do what one can," he answered, and took his candle and disappeared.

I lay still, smoking, and the flame of the candle quivered in the draught. Then I knew, beyond any shadow of doubt, that the thing I had contemplated doing would have to be done. If one ponders a project long enough, a time arrives when the intensity of one's thought renders action inevitable, and I knew that I had reached this point. I felt weak and fearful, but I knew that I had to act, and at once, and that the days I had been living, which were but as a succession of dreams, were over, and that the Change of which I had had so many premonitions was upon me.

BOOK IV

§ 1

I *KNOW* now that I can continue to live like this no longer. Who is this man Victor that he should not know the ruin he has wrought in my life? He shall know—he shall know everything, and I will demand from him all that of which he has robbed me. I will go to him, and it will be well for him to answer me without subtlety or evasion, for I shall carry a weapon concealed about me, and unless he restores the life he has stolen, he shall pay for it with his own. This is the project that has been seething and shaping in my mind, and I know now that this passive life of mine is over and that I have to act. I shall stand before him and he shall know the secret that the years and the silence have shared with me. Yes, he shall know of the wilderness into which he has driven me and out of which I have returned, strong with the strength of my suffering and armed with the weapons of hatred.

By God, he shall listen to me! He shall hear every count in my indictment against him. I will reveal to him how he first of all woke in me that spirit which questioned and doubted all the joys of earth until the garden of the world became an arid wilderness. Ah, and more! he shall know how he awoke in my soul a dream as high as the stars that ever goaded my weariness to seek in the wilderness for the shadow of its beauty. He has robbed me of earth and then not allowed me to mourn my loss in the dust, because of the dream he created in my soul—which whispered that from the sepulchre of earth I should see some miracle of resurrection. Let him not seek to interrupt me! Hatred shall be my inspiration, and the memory of my wrongs shall lend me eloquence. In my memory there is an inventory of all that of which he has robbed me, and he shall recompense me for every item there recorded.

With what shall I not charge him when at last we stand together, face to face? I shall say to him: "Strength was mine, and by reason of that strength the prizes of the world were within reach of my hand; but as I stretched forth my hand to take my own, you spoke one word and my arm fell nerveless to my side. And again I looked towards another horizon, and on some summit, not too far removed, I saw the prize my ambition coveted, and with eager steps I began to climb. But when I was separated by only a stride from my crown, the shadow of your thought descended, and lo! I saw but a bauble too slight even to give away."

What shall I not say to him? I shall say:

"I loved Life with so intense a love that it made a fire of my blood. So great was this love that when ambition was taken from me, I could laugh with joy at the knowledge of all that I still possessed. It was an ecstasy to me to remember all the infinite number of things that I could seize and make mine. But whenever I stooped to pluck a flower, a chill came over me and, half turning, I saw beside me the shadow of your mind; and when I looked again at the flower, it had withered, and my desire for it had died. You have robbed me of every desire of my heart.

"Before you came into my life, I knew a passion to create things of beauty out of my thoughts and dreams, so deep in its intensity that it whispered to me that I could erect—here on earth—an invisible temple of beauty in which my soul might find sanctuary. And out of my dreams and thoughts I started to build a temple of words, so that I might forget all the squalor and the drab realities of life. And again the shadow of your thought fell across the heaven of my dream, and I knew that the temple I was building was founded on fear, and that only a lie could dwell therein.

"And I turned from all these things of which your shadow had robbed me, and there was a bitterness in my heart. Then I determined that I would find a way to forget you, and all that you represented, and that, as you had thwarted me in the invisible worlds of ambition and love, I would escape from you in the actual world where one can see and touch and hold. So I gave full freedom to my desire for women, determined to find joy beyond the reach of your forbidding shadow and a midnight consolation for all that the day had denied. I promised myself that if you had denied me all that my soul desired, my body should find a consolation outside the sphere of your withering presence. But I found that I shrank from the arms that were eager to enfold me, and those that were stretched towards me in love were but an entrance to a temple wherein I heard again the sound of your voice. It mattered not where I sought, for, everywhere, I found you, until all earth seemed but an echo of your voice."

Will he sit silent through all the fury of the charges that I must thunder against him? Shall I not appear to him not only as a stranger, but a madman? I do not know, and I do not care. He is the thief of thieves. Any one who robs another of his thought robs him of a world. Why should I not slay him? Not only has he crippled my feet, that once were swift in the race of life, but he has robbed my heart of the desire for any of the prizes that are the spoils of the victorious. When I go to him to demand what is mine, I shall go prepared to strike.

And yet, why is it that I am fearful? One part of me is afraid of the resolution at which I have arrived. It is terrible to think that all the secrecy of the years is to end, and that I am about to reveal myself before him in all my nakedness. Besides, can he ever recompense me for all that of which he has defrauded me? Does it lie in his power? Am I not in the position of a man who has lent great sums to another, which he has squandered, and now is not my remedy but to make him bankrupt? Revenge, I may have, but restitution—restitution? Can he plant again that which he has torn up by the roots? I do not know. I ask—and nothing answers. I only know that I am impelled to action by a force which is more powerful than reason, and that the days of my old life are numbered. But I would not continue to live like this, even if I could, for my very thoughts are his thoughts and my very dreams are but the many shadows of his single vision. I vacillate between a passion of hatred for him and a passionate desire for death. At one moment I seek to annihilate and at the next I crave annihilation.

§ 2

Shall I go to him by night, or shall I strike with my fist on his door in the splendour of some sunset hour? How I dramatize my determination and seek to realize all its implications by varying the background upon which it will be enacted! My imagination strives to picture him. I feel that when his door yields to me and I enter his room, I shall find him at work on his book, several passages of which I have been destined to hear. He will see but a stranger, and I shall see my destiny. A strange meeting! O God, how incomprehensible is the world! And how lonely, lost, and isolated is each individual in all this multitude of human beings! But this I know, that once I have seen him, my life in this house is over. Where I shall go and what new ironies of mischance await me, I cannot guess, but the drama of my life is about to change its setting. A curtain is about to drop, and I am afraid.

§ 3

I will set down here the last words of Victor's that I shall ever record. Let them be written here, and then I must hasten to do swiftly what I know has to be done. . . .

A great peace has come to me, filling all my being with a spacious certainty, and I know what I am—I know what I have to do, and I know that I am not alone. It matters not greatly if I fall again for a season into the chaos from which I have emerged, for I have seen the glory of earth and know that it is but the shadow of the thought of God. And the meaning of all my life is in this moment, for in this moment I am born and the darkness falls from me like a dream. It is enough. I know not where I shall wander; I know not those who are coming to seek me, nor those to whom I am hastening, nor do I care to know, for at last I have a talisman to tell me where my place is, and to reveal to me those to whom I belong. I have deciphered Life's signature. Nothing is changed, yet everything is new. I was deaf and now I hear. I was blind and now I see. This moment is given to me so that it may enter into me and become mine, and then I can go my way into the highways of life, to dwell there with men and women, and share my secret with all those who are not hypnotized by the lie of death. There is a song in my soul, and I know that it was sung before the creation of the world.

§ 4

It is over! The tragedy, the farce, is finished! The lights are out, and like a madman I rave in the darkness on an empty stage. Is the auditorium thronged with ghosts? Do the phantoms of my thoughts sit perched in the invisible stalls? Do the wraiths of old imaginings gaze listlessly down from circles and galleries? Do I face a spectral audience eager to witness the final catastrophe of illusion before it breaks forth into mocking laughter and derisive applause? By the God of heaven, I will anticipate them! See! I, too, am laughing! I am seized with uncontrollable laughter that wakes shrill echoes in every nook and corner of this mad, rickety house. I will address this phantom audience—though no call for author has come from the dark silence. "Ladies and gentlemen! What I intended for a tragedy has turned into a farce, it seems; but I have an excuse to offer you. I wrote this play in my sleep. Yes, I assure you, it is only a dream, and now—I am awake. But I have more to tell you, and I counsel you to listen to me earnestly. The play I have offered to you is the greatest of dramas, for it reveals that life itself is nothing but a tedious scene in a tragic farce. With all due modesty, ladies and gentlemen (or phantoms and spectres, if you will)—with all due modesty, I must assure you that I am like God, for I have created a play without a meaning, and He has created a world without a plot. The difference between us is that now I am awake, while He still creates from the depths of His dream. I beg each one of you to search the inner recesses of your lives, and you will then discover just such a drama as the one I have had the honour to present to you to-night. You remain silent, ladies and gentlemen; can it possibly be that you understand me? Search your lives, that is all I beg of you, and you will discover just such a drama as the one you have witnessed to-night. And now, ladies and gentlemen, will you withdraw, please? All the emergency exits are open, and another night, less real than this darkness, awaits you outside. The author would spend a contemplative half-hour alone with his broken tragedy. He would gather up the fragments, pack them up, for he hopes to produce a new version of this play in the next world. Even if it had proved a success in this one, which it has not, he had no intention of putting it up for a run here. For he feels that, if he has a theme at all, it is concerned with Eternity and, therefore, it would necessarily appear a little ridiculous amid the shows of Time! I thank you, ghosts and spectres, for one thing only—your silence. Good-night! the curtain falls, and I vanish."

§ 5

Somehow I must be calm—even now I must attempt to be calm. But in any event, a few pages and I have finished, and the pen will fall from my hand. . . .

It was an autumn day. Just such a day as that upon which I first heard Victor's voice on the stairs. All day long I had lingered by the window, looking out at the people passing in the streets below. The day had passed like a mute pageant. I had not thought about Victor—I had not thought about anything. But just as the first shadows of dusk fell into my room, I left the window, and suddenly, like a flash of lightning, I knew that the moment had arrived, and that now—now!—I would go to Victor and demand back from him the life he had stolen.

I remember that I trembled, and that a sickening sense of weakness possessed me. My mind supplied countless reasons why the moment was utterly inopportune, and though I played mentally with each excuse, I knew that I should go, and that delay was only needless torture. Moreover, I knew with an absolute certainty that Victor was in his room, for only a few minutes earlier I had heard him reading a passage from his book.

The hour had struck. My secret life was over.

I tried desperately to conjure up that fierce, passionate spirit within me, so that a frenzy of hatred might give me the strength of fanaticism, but it was not to be invoked by any arbitrary act of my will. The shadows were beginning to deepen, and I knew that I could not delay much longer. I lingered, fidgeting about the room, touching this, looking at that, but with no sense of actuality. And then, when I had despaired of the aid of passion, suddenly I was stung to fierce resentment and hatred. So this was the state to which this man had reduced me! This shivering, nerve-wracked, indefinite creature was his work! This clown who had no place in life, no work to do, no hope to lure him through the labyrinth of days and nights! By God, he should answer to me—and now! I slipped a weapon into my pocket, and with murder in my heart I went noisily out of my room into the passage. For some reason the silence infuriated me, and, raising my fist, I hammered three times on his door. The startled echoes of the old house woke, lamented, and died away. Silence—deeper than ever—older than night. Why did he not answer? His silence was the ultimate insult.

Again I struck the door, and kicked it in impotent fury, calling him by his name, and demanding that he should open to me. There was no sound, and suddenly I realized that he was afraid. A triumphant laugh broke from me, and a sense of power such as I have never known swept through me. All hesitation, all weakness, fell from me, and I knew that at last I was myself again, and that the old life I had known was all about me, waiting to welcome me. I felt a desire to prolong this moment, so that the intoxication of this new sense of power might enter into me so deeply that I might never again be without the assurance of its audacity. I laughed again and again, while my mind gloated over the thought of the man's fear the other side of the locked door. But soon anger returned, and I shouted to him to open, or I would burst the door down and strike him dead at my feet. Still silence. I flung myself at the door, and to my delight it seemed to yield a little. Again and yet again I flung myself against it with the whole of my weight. It shook on its hinges, and the old house seemed to creak and sway on its foundations. Then, with a superlative effort, I literally hurled myself at the door, and with a deafening crash it fell bodily to the floor. With a cry of triumph, I entered the room.

It was empty.

Gasping for breath, strangely elated, I tried to see where he was hiding; but the shadows of dusk half filled the room, and my very excitement made it impossible for me to rivet my attention on anything. Besides, I knew now that he was frightened, that he was so frightened that he had hidden himself, and at that discovery all my pride burst into flame and I felt the intoxication of a god.

How long I enjoyed this triumph, I do not know, but suddenly

I realized that the room had grown dark, and that I must hasten to my revenge. All thought of flinging my indictment in his teeth had vanished. I had only one aim—to discover his hiding-place and to strike him dead. The frenzy of the murderer was singing its terrible song in my heart, and to strike and to kill were the only joys in the world. But the darkness was shielding him, and I was in a strange room. With a terrible effort, I restrained my triumph, and sought for matches in the darkness. At last, after a search which seemed to occupy hours, my groping hand discovered them, and by their aid I found a candle, which I lit and placed on a table. Then I turned to survey the room.

It was an attic, and most of the walls were surrounded by bookcases, one of which had been brought to the ground by the breaking in of the door. By the quavering, indefinite light of the candle I could discern a table and a couch, but little else. The silence could be felt. For a second the shadow of a nameless fear crossed my heart. I cried his name aloud, summoned him from his hiding-place; but the sound of my own voice seemed unfamiliar, and no answer came from the shadowed gloom of the room. My fury became dumb, and mechanically I turned to examine this attic. By now I was more accustomed to the dim half-light. At length I stood before his table. It was covered with manuscript, and his pen had rolled to the side. It was obvious that I had disturbed him while he was seated at work.

Then—even now I don't know why—I was consumed with curiosity to know what he was writing at the actual moment I had beaten on his door. I took up the sheet of paper, and carried it to the light of the flickering candle. A cry broke from me. *I recognized my own handwriting!* What ghastly joke was this? Again I peered narrowly. Yes, it was my own hand. I strove to read what was written there, but the words held no meaning for me. A moan of despair broke from me, and I began to tremble violently. A sense of wild terror encompassed me, and I felt a cold perspiration on my forehead. The sheet fluttered from my hand to the floor, and all the room seemed full of ironical whisperings and derisive laughter. With a supreme effort I rallied my forces and looked round me. Then I noticed several candles on a bookshelf, and, seizing them, I lit them rapidly, one after the other, putting them down haphazard about the room. Then I looked about me, and immediately a cry broke from me, and fear was like ice in my blood.

I was in my own room!

I know not how long I stood there like one petrified, but I remember that I rushed to the table, and with trembling hands examined the manuscripts lying upon it. There were two piles, each in my own handwriting. One was the manuscript of this book, and by its side was the manuscript of another work. I turned the latter over, but could make no sense of what was written there. Then I saw that certain passages appearing in this mysterious work had also been copied into the first manuscript. My heart stopped beating. What was the meaning, the explanation? Was this madness?—was this what men call madness? I rushed towards the door that I had broken in, and with difficulty I lifted it and leant it against the wall. I saw that, *on the inside*, it was completely covered by a bookcase, from which most of the volumes had fallen. One could have lived in the room for years without knowing that a door was hidden behind that bookcase.

I crept back into the room. And the mocking voices surged round me like an invisible chorus, and malicious laughter scourged my trembling soul. Then all my thoughts narrowed to one issue— flight! With a curse on my lips, I rushed out of the room, down the endless flights of stairs, feeling that a host of spectres pursued me, and at last reached the bottom, when I saw my landlord awaiting me. He seemed to be trembling, and his face was white with fear. I seized him roughly by the shoulder.

"Tell me where he is," I cried, "or I will kill you. The man in the room next to mine—Victor! Tell me where he is, for I will kill him to-night. God cannot prevent it."

He fell back from me with a gesture of repulsion.

"You are ill," he muttered.

"The man who lives next to me!" I shouted. "The man who has robbed me of life itself—the man who has stolen the world from me—where is he? where is he?"

He looked at me narrowly. "But you are mad," he cried. "There is only your room on the top floor. There is no room next to yours. How could there be? You have been there alone."

I flung him from me with a bitter laugh. . . .

And then suddenly, in an instant, the whole of my being was illuminated, and I knew in the depths of me a certainty deeper than the foundations of the world.

I went out slowly into the night. The silence could be felt, and the whole of the heavens blazed with the glory of the stars.

ALSO AVAILABLE FROM VALANCOURT BOOKS

MICHAEL ARLEN	Hell! said the Duchess
R. C. ASHBY (RUBY FERGUSON)	He Arrived at Dusk
FRANK BAKER	The Birds
WALTER BAXTER	Look Down in Mercy
CHARLES BEAUMONT	The Hunger and Other Stories
DAVID BENEDICTUS	The Fourth of June
PAUL BINDING	Harmonica's Bridegroom
CHARLES BIRKIN	The Smell of Evil
JOHN BLACKBURN	A Scent of New-Mown Hay
THOMAS BLACKBURN	A Clip of Steel
	The Feast of the Wolf
JOHN BRAINE	Room at the Top
	The Vodi
MICHAEL CAMPBELL	Lord Dismiss Us
R. CHETWYND-HAYES	The Monster Club
BASIL COPPER	The Great White Space
	Necropolis
HUNTER DAVIES	Body Charge
JENNIFER DAWSON	The Ha-Ha
BARRY ENGLAND	Figures in a Landscape
RONALD FRASER	Flower Phantoms
GILLIAN FREEMAN	The Liberty Man
	The Leather Boys
	The Leader
STEPHEN GILBERT	The Landslide
	The Burnaby Experiments
	Ratman's Notebooks
MARTYN GOFF	The Youngest Director
STEPHEN GREGORY	The Cormorant
F. L. GREEN	Odd Man Out
JOHN HAMPSON	Saturday Night at the Greyhound
THOMAS HINDE	The Day the Call Came
CLAUDE HOUGHTON	I Am Jonathan Scrivener
	This Was Ivor Trent
CYRIL KERSH	The Aggravations of Minnie Ashe
GERALD KERSH	Fowlers End
	Nightshade and Damnations
FRANCIS KING	Never Again

Lightning Source UK Ltd.
Milton Keynes UK
UKOW03f0710210414

230302UK00002B/20/P